Illustrated by:
Diana Naneva

DESSI NIKKO

ALICE
ON A
FRIDAY
NIGHT

Alice on a Friday Night was first published in Bulgarian in 2016 and was granted the Bulgarian National Prize for Debut Literature.

This first English edition is published with the financial support of the National Culture Fund, Bulgaria.

Paperback: ISBN 978-619-7643-27-5
Ebook: ISBN 978-619-7643-26-8

Translated by: Dessi Nikko, Alexander Marinov
Edited by: Claire Stephens
Illustrated by: Diana Naneva
Illustration on p. 248 by: Dahlia Besedin
Cover photography by: Mira Nedyalkova

Published by: Words on the Water

To my family.
Thanks for giving me
the hands I needed
so I could give myself wings.

Special thanks to:
Reni Yankova
Marina Yaneva
Kossara Baharova

INTRO

I'm Alice. But Alice in reverse. First I shattered all the mirrors I could find in the Looking-Glass World. Then I crashed into Wonderland, eager to meet every mad hatter, every shade of insanity, and creep through seven years of bad luck for every mirror I'd broken.

The wonders of the land bring me comfort. But will I ever find my way out of the dark rabbit hole?

This is a story about seeking and finding.

As kids we know all the answers. Then we grow up. Forget. Become obsessed with searching for Meaning.

And while searching we get totally lost.

I don't know if the crisis of being 24 is an officially recognized thing, but that's definitely what I'm going through. My childhood determination has vanished along the way. Now I tumble between all and nothing in every possible aspect. I plan for the past, all the while regretting the tremendous mistakes I might make in the future. This could be good though. Maybe people who are well-balanced in the middle of their lives – those who are spared from a midlife crisis – have simply dealt with their personality issues earlier on.

Friday night.

Here I am again, full of resolve to put my life in order. Naturally, I start with my closet. Decisions to tidy up our chaos often begin with tidying up our clothes. Too bad that's usually where the project ends too.

I fold one thing after another, unable to decide what to get rid of. Then I don't feel like tidying up anymore. I head for the sofa instead, a glass of whiskey in hand.

"Any hope for you to stop fooling around and get to writing your book?"

"Hope dies last but mine's in a coma already," I say in a dark interpretation of the cotton-candy cliché. This brings out the familiar sparkle in Annie's laughter. Few can laugh the way she does. Most people are too self-conscious, and hers is a shriek of untamed emotions. She mixes all available sounds in her euphoric hysteria. PFRRSS-MHOO-MHOO-GHE-KE-KE-CHSHEE-HEE-HEE-HEE. Something like that.

The night we first met, Annie laughed wildly as well. It was the summer after my high school graduation. I'd heard a lot about her and her sisters. Urban legends described them as savage sirens who'd clasp their long arms around you the moment you came close, whirling you about in their dangerous grip ever so fiercely until everything grew frightful. Beautiful things were also frightful with Annie, for they weren't actually real. Eventually you became something monstrous and shocking… Then you ceased to exist.

Annie was hard to find. You couldn't get in touch with her or her sisters on a whim; someone had to hook you up.

A friend of mine hooked me up.

"Make a wish," Annie told me on that first night together. She commands effortlessly, morphing the imperative into an informatively seductive whisper: "You're making a wish-sh-sh."

So a wish I made.

"What did you ask for?"

"Well … it's supposed to be a secret, isn't it?"

"Bullshit. If you want something, you need to say it out loud. Now tell me what you wished for."

Once again, I obeyed.

"Good. Now let's see if it'll come true. Heads or tails?"

"Heads!" I always choose heads. I believe it comes up more often.

"Look at the moon now. Is it heads or tails?"

"It's tails. So my wish won't come true after all…"

"Of course it will."

"But the moon's clearly showing tails…"

"Yeah. Making your wish come true depends on you though, not on the moon. And if you can see heads or tails in the sky, you can do anything."

Everything Annie says makes sense. At first her ideas resemble some trendy crap about positive thinking, but her arguments are different, mostly cynical. She knows how to use all the nice rosy words that everyone loves, and she knows how to use the other words too. The genuine ones. Annie doesn't fake her optimism. You can tell she's suffered through it.

"Remember your wish from the night we met?"

As usual, our thoughts are on the same frequency.

"I wished to become a writer."

"Yeah, only writers don't *become*; they just *write*."

Of course I know that. When I was a kid I did actually write. In sixth grade, I used to treat my friends to chapters from my "first novel," an adventure story. Then I grew up. I stopped writing and started dreaming about becoming a writer instead.

"Why did you stop?"

Oh, the endless reasons an author could produce to answer that question! Once, I spent three months suppressing my inspiration for a fairy tale just because I didn't have a notebook beautiful enough for it.

"Even if I do write a good book, there's no way everybody will like it. There'll be people insulting my work!"

Annie doesn't buy the excuse.

"Do you like every single book you read? Maybe authors should go and kill themselves just because they don't suit your taste?"

"I get your point, okay? But when it comes to my work, I'll forget the comforting shit…"

"Don't sweat it, I'll be there to remind you. Any other excuses for not writing?"

"I don't know anything. What could I possibly tell people?"

"Oh come on. You're a smart girl, Alice."

I really hate it when someone says that. A smart girl. What does that even mean?

"I'm only smart in theory," I say, "in reality, my life is a mess. There's never enough Time, and with ticket and fuel prices Space has become too much as well. I struggle with all the philosophical concepts! When I start wondering where the Universe ends, or if it ends at all, I get dizzy and I… What time is it?"

The unexpected question catches Annie off guard. However, she's quick to reply,

"10:22."

"Just like I thought! It couldn't be anything else."

Annie throws question marks in the air.

"Just read the numbers the way they're showing on the display," I prompt.

"22:22… So?"

"So! Lately I've been seeing repeating numbers all the time: missed calls on my phone at 23:23, texts at 07:07, all the other hours and minutes with repeating numbers, bills with repeating numbers, license plates with repeating numbers… 22:22, in particular, shows up almost every night! And other people tell me they've noticed it too. It's not like I believe in signs and all that shit but I'm starting to wonder whether there could be something here… I've got no idea what exactly is going on, but there's something with the numbers! I'm clueless, and here you want me to write a book!"

A mysterious smile on her face.

"The repeating numbers, eh? Interesting. I know what they mean but I want you to figure it out on your own."

Of course she knows. She always knows everything. I beg for more information but Annie only drops smirks into my empty cupped hands.

"Putting this enigmatic stuff aside, I can't make sense of everyday life either," I say. "It's full of obvious absurdity! And what gets me the most is how people brush their teeth, go to work, and have dinner in total oblivion, not paying attention to all the injustice!"

"Injustice?"

"In this bizarre world of ours, some people call their belongings 'baby.' Others throw their real babies in the trash. We often react to pregnancy as if someone were dying. This is a world where clowns, dolls and music boxes strike horror, instead of bringing joy to children – which is their original purpose, right? And the other way around: vampires, devils and other villains are supposed to be terrifying but recently they're incarnated in the bodies of beautiful actors. Kids want to be just like them.

"We're not cruel, we say; we only do cruel things when obeying a bad person's orders. Yet, if a petite dictator told us to help people instead of sending them off to concentration camps, we'd laugh in his face. We'd readily disobey that. What we fail to understand is that the most dangerous people aren't the ones who've been proven bad. Those who don't have the balls to be officially mean are even more repulsive. They torture children, animals and women because they can't stand up to their equals. Even murderers despise such scumbags. Still, in this strange world of ours, children and animals are tortured on a regular basis. It's not only the TV-news examples. There are so many everyday details that go unnoticed, like the old ladies who scold kids for picking flowers from their gardens. Sometimes the kids even get smacked. But they never mean to kill flowers, they just want to bring something colorful and beautiful home to mommy. She, on the other hand, shouts at them if they happen to ruin her lipstick. Sometimes she even slaps them! But kids don't ruin lipstick – they only draw pictures, or want to try on makeup to be gorgeous like mommy.

"The concept of beauty is also distorted. Women deliberately stifle their smiles to avoid wrinkles. Dusty plastic plants are referred to as 'decorations,' and deadly animal fights are called 'entertainment.' And why on earth do we produce candy and all kinds of food in the shape of cute animals? So that we can bite their heads off with pleasure? Isn't it sick?! Eating meat is fine, I think; it's not against nature, but all the other atrocities we commit against animals are. No amount of vegetarianism can ever make up for that!

"Mankind's specialty is pointing out how we're much more intelligent than all the other species around, but really we can only admire them for surviving on the same planet with idiots like us. Still, in this messed up world of ours, you can be on the verge of giving up on human values and pseudo-intelligence, but then you spot an airplane in the sky and – *whoosh!* – your faith in humanity is suddenly restored."

I clap to show my enthusiasm about planes. Annie isn't impressed. You know those special women who don't look ridiculous with short hair? Moreover, they appear so deliciously attractive that it makes you long to absorb everything, all their juices, gestures and words; your own worldview seems dull in comparison. Well, Annie's just like those chicks. And right now she's obviously bored with my lengthy complaint.

"Airplanes," she says, "were invented by someone who was practical, not merely an idealist and a dreamer. You won't even make it to the nearest intersection if you keep banging your head against the absurdities of society. You'd better tell your own story, and tell it simply."

"But I want to find answers! What would people learn from a book where I tell them about myself?"

A roll of Annie's eerie, all-seeing eyes.

"Your readers can find ready-to-consume answers on Google. The rest they want to discover themselves. People don't chase mathematically correct answers in art, Alice. They're after points of view that remind them they have their own point of view..." Annie's nail fondles my cheek. "If you want to have a point of view, you just need to observe. And to have a point, of course. You do observe, so obviously what you're missing is the point. I'll give you one right now: tell me about Friday night."

"Friday night? How is Friday night even a point?"

"On a Friday night you can tell the most about people. That's when workaholics still work. Jealous people fight. Those who are newly in love are most affectionate, while long-term partners go for boys' or girls' nights out. Devoted moms stay home with their kids... Writers often deviate from their original thoughts, but as long as you always come back to Friday Night you'll be just fine."

I won't be coming back anywhere 'cause I'm not going anywhere, I wanna say, but Annie waves my objection away before I can open my mouth.

"You people are afraid to go after your dreams. So what if some of them prove unattainable? That's the sexiest part. Otherwise, you wouldn't have dreams anymore, you'd end up with nothing but fulfilled stuff."

A pause, although she's clearly not finished yet. I already know how Annie is — once she's off in a certain direction she dives to the very bottom, then comes back up and insists on squeezing every last drop out. In a moment she takes off again.

"Not every fulfilled dream brings happiness, Alice. If it fails to make you strong, success can make you terribly vulnerable."

At last she seems satisfied with my initiation in all that matters in life. She carries on in a purr:

"Don't be afraid, Alice! Write! Writers are what they are because they think, because they create, not because people read them. Don't fear not knowing. There's charm in writing and asking questions, Alice.

Just write!"

So that's what I do.

First, I write about my trip to Signland. I fill page after page, hour after hour. It goes so easy, having Annie around – I'm suddenly more focused, confident in the quality of my words. Inspired by her presence, ideas flood my mind like never before. I want to collect them all in a bucket, and I desperately try to write everything down but the rain grows

stronger…

and stronger…

Every single drop is amazing, or at least I think it is. The impossibility of catching all that genius in the bucket is frustrating. The bucket

brims over…

then overflows.

Eventually I decide it's time to go to bed. Morning's here yet it feels like midnight to me. My body doesn't register the need to sleep, but my mind is tired of collecting ideas. I can finish the Signland story later.

Cuddling my teddy bear, I will my eyelids to shut.

That's right, I sleep with a teddy bear. He's very wholesome and he makes me feel comfy. My waking hours though, are all spent with Boro – my fluffy toy rabbit. Unlike the teddy, Boro is bad. Fire brings him to life and people say ours is a toxic relationship. I don't care, I love him. He's a magic wand: I take him between my fingers and all of a sudden everything has more Meaning. My lips close around him and nothing can really upset me anymore. With Boro, even waiting at the bus stop doesn't feel passive. I take him everywhere with me. If he's not around I start losing my mind. He's small; fits in a 5.5 by 8.5 cm box… The Meaning of life contained in a 5.5 by 8.5 box!

All night long Boro has been by my side but now the last magic wand is nearing its end. I don't have a reason to stay awake anymore. Annie watches over my sleep. But sleep is not really sleep when I'm with her. I find myself in some sort of a hazy transitional state. Semi-sleep. Neither awake, nor dreaming. Dreamlike visions infested with awareness of every sound, every movement in the real world around me.

Eventually I semi-wake up. Annie is gone, only her taste still lingering on my tongue. I leave my apartment to find Boro.

A week later I finish the story.

Signland

I went there on a work-and-travel program for university students.

On the poorly-signed streets back home, in the East, in the Balkans, time is coffee. It's hot and it's strong. Not too much milk in it, preferably with thick cream. Signland is a different story. Here, time is money. I'm not saying you can't buy yourself a coffee. Of course you can. You can even choose between loads of different flavored creamers. But then the drink of your choice is poured into a practical cup with a lid – a to-go cup – because you're supposed to be making money, so you drink on-the-go. Well, this is no way to have coffee! This is simply consuming it. There's a mellow philosophy behind drinking coffee and people in Signland are clearly not familiar with it. Or they've deliberately forgotten it.

Short story short, this country's past goes like this:

Smart, enterprising, innovative people sailed here on their ships. They weren't quite sure where they'd sailed to, but it didn't matter so much at the time. What mattered was that a huge portion of the native population was wiped out, and plenty of space was freed. Maybe it was this very act of freeing that gave birth to the smart, enterprising, innovative settlers' love for the word "freedom." Smart as they were, they soon figured that the newly-freed space could be filled with the native population of yet another continent. This other native population could even be enslaved to work for them! Then the smartasses started killing each other over the question of whether it was better to keep the native population of this other continent as slaves, or if it was more innovative to grant them freedom.

"Off with their heads!" screeched the Queen of Hearts.

"Freedom, free-e-do-om!" commanded Her Majesty Constitution, the Queen of Signs.

Eventually, Constitution won the Civil War. Little by little, all the slaves were freed. From then on, the North and the South decided to bet on teamwork and the smart, enterprising, innovative people's empire flourished. Excluding the moments of depression, of course. Perhaps that's when the Signlanders' love for "psychotherapy" was conceived. People began turning to psychotherapy all the time, even when their pet hamsters died. Prescriptions for happy pills joined the vast artillery of signs guiding life in this seemingly orderly country.

Almost everyone in the world started imitating the smart, enterprising, innovative people who, in turn, started poking their noses (and the noses of their jet fighters) in almost everyone else's business. They kept putting signs all over their land until the need to think on your own completely disappeared.

"Man, the more developed a city in the modern world is, the higher the number of creeps there are lurking around!" a friend of mine once said. I couldn't agree more.

One Friday night in Signland all I wanted was to drink a cup of coffee and chill.

Drowsily, orderly, in compliance with all the signs around – that's how I'd spent the whole day that Friday. Just like every other day since Chris, my travel buddy from uni, and I became certified lifeguards across the ocean. We'd quickly learned that whatever difficulty we encountered in this country could be solved by a quick look around. Sure enough, there'd be some directions telling us exactly what we were expected to do.

Most Signlanders are oh-so-polite, no argument there. Overly polite, even, when they think you don't fully grasp what's written on a particular sign. Always eager to clarify. If you're looking for an address nearby, many will be glad to give you a ride there. If you ask them to overlook the smallest detail of a rule, they'll make it clear – most politely so – that such unholiness is out of the question. Their politeness seems to wear thin only when you have the arrogance to insist on deviating from the Canon of Signs.

As we didn't have a car, one of our polite fellow lifeguards spared us from walking the long distance to the swimming pool every day. As usual, he arrived that morning to pick us up with reggaeton blasting from his car speakers. He proudly declared himself a Puerto Rican. Never tired of telling stories about all the reggaeton celebrities he'd partied with, the Puerto Rican way. He was cool; acknowledged that sometimes it was right to break the rules. The Signlanders' "Rules rule!" slogan made him miss Puerto Rico even more.

Work was fine that day. Before we opened the pool for the public, Boss had us line up to make sure we were geared up to perfection. Visor or hat. Shades. Whistle. Swimsuit. T-shirt and shorts over the swimsuit – a must for the girls, too much skin couldn't be exposed. First-aid kit on the waist. Duct tape on the feet for those who had warts.

"Okay!"

Boss had some news, too: there was an ongoing state-wide audit and all public pools were flooded by civil lifeguard inspectors. I pictured them ducking behind bushes on the neighboring mini-golf course, stopwatches clutched in their hands. Why stopwatches? Let me explain.

In order to be certified as a lifeguard in Signland, you needed to receive special training. Fair enough. Among other things, it was mandatory to master the different types of "scanning systems" for localizing potential victims. The most common technique was known as "The Full Arc Scan with Pronounced Downward Head Swing and a Bump." No kidding. This is a quote from the lifeguard manual, only without the descriptive illustration. Translated into human, the whole concept is: you're so fired if you stop rotating your head like crazy, and each rotation should last 15 seconds exactly. Hence the crucial need for stopwatches.

Lucky me, the stopwatch seemed to like me. I nailed a scan time of exactly 15 seconds, and not a millisecond more. Lots of praise. A big colorful bead for special merit – they put those on our whistle cords. Yay, I was a truly professional lifeguard! Right… Only I wasn't. If you ask a really good swimmer, "How long can you swim for?" their reply should be "Days!" (also quoted from said manual). I couldn't swim for days and I was pretty sure there was absolutely no chance I could rescue another soul in water deeper than my own height. Fortunately, I had more common sense than the civil inspectors and their stopwatches. If it was up to them, they would've assigned me to some deep void with a wave machine just because my scan time was okay. I opted to work at a facility with shallow pools instead. It was safe enough, as long as I didn't fall asleep and fail to notice the toddlers who splashed face down in the water. They did that a lot. Then they'd start waving their little limbs about helplessly, so I was really doing my best to stay alert.

Overall we did "Amazing!" on the civil inspection. Boss was so psyched. Honored us with a patriotic speech before we closed the pool for the night. The other lifeguards, all hyped up too, tried to drag Chris and me to a party dedicated to our triumph. We were cherished guests at their parties, and no wonder. In Signland most people who work as lifeguards are either Eastern European university students or local high schoolers. Guess who was in charge of providing booze for the parties.

It goes without saying that teenagers in Signland are more prone to neglecting the signs. When it comes to getting wasted, this proclivity is twice as powerful as the fear of "no phone for two weeks," their parents' favorite punishment.

The underage lifeguards' post-audit shopping list:
- four six-packs of charmingly cheap and disgustingly tasteless beer
- tequila
- a cobalt blue bottle of vodka

We got them everything but decided to join the celebration later, and only briefly. As Chris pointed out, we'd be the only adults present and if the police came they could lock us up. A most likely scenario. Neighbors in Signland enjoy calling the cops as soon as they hear a commotion underway.

The get-together was to take place in the backyard of one of the girls.

"Just come with me, guys!" she said. She couldn't see why we needed to go to our place for a shower and a change of clothes. She wore sport shorts, a sweatshirt with her school crest, silver heels, and a matching purse.

Regardless of the fashionista's opinion we insisted on going home. That wasn't an easy task though. In Signland you're doomed if you don't have a car. You can't even get to the shop on the corner of the street because there's no shop on the corner of the street. Just neighborhoods packed with nice white houses, exactly like those shown in the movies, only on screen you don't realize that there's nothing around but the houses and a variety of churches. If you want to go shopping, you need to get to a shopping center. Plain and simple. We got a ride there for the booze mission, but then our Puerto Rican's car disappeared in the direction of the party, and our trip home was left to the whims of fate.

At least we knew the shopping center well – we had to do all kinds of stuff there. My personal favorite – laundry. You'd sit down, eyes peeled for laundry thieves, making sure your dirty clothes didn't disappear; meanwhile, intimidating-looking guys gathered around, staring and wishing the clothes on your body *would* disappear.

There were many intimidating-looking guys in the area where we lived.

"Where are you staying?" Boss's wife had asked when she picked us up from the airport on our arrival.

"Close to Seven Corners. We saw on Google Maps that the pool's there and searched for a place nearby."

Seven Corners. The name had a nostalgic ring to us – a reminder of The Five Corners back home, one of the landmark spots in our city. I imagine people often try to find such similarities when they're far away from their home country.

"Good Lord! That neighborhood's packed with immigrants!" Boss's wife had exclaimed in terror, expressly warning Chris to never let me walk alone there after sunset. *Hold your horses a sec, ma'am! What happened to political correctness? Not judging people by their ethnicity?* If I said something like that, she'd want to tar and feather me on the spot. Plus, Boss's wife clearly didn't realize we came from the Wild East. Guys with wife beaters and fan knives were something we were pretty used to.

But certain characters around Seven Corners did prove to be a challenge. The gods of vulgar remarks on the street, they made me feel naked, so naked that I was sure I'd never get my hands on any clothes again for the rest of my life. They frequented the pool, some sporting their MS-13 tattoos. Once a guy with a particularly high number of particularly ugly tattoos started arguing with me. I cut him off rudely and then, still pissed off about the unpleasant experience, wrote about it to my sister back home. Sis responded instantly and told me NEVER to do that again: MS-13 stood for Mara Salvatrucha, one of the world's most notorious gangs, and its members were VERY dangerous. "What does 13 stand for?" I texted back. Sis called me straight away to shout at me that she was dead serious. Well, how was I supposed to know these things? Come to think of it, three minutes after the Mara Salvatrucha-tattooed guys would arrive at the pool, a police officer would show up as well; apparently Boss called the cops for our protection. I'd thought it was just another useless precaution. During my stay in Signland, I always found it hard to tell whether there was any real danger, or it was just the Signlanders' imagination.

Abandoned there, right in the heart of Seven Corners, Chris and I came up with a slick strategy to avoid the long walk back to our place. We bought brand new bikes from Target. We could return them the next day, no need for explanations, and get a full refund. I was tempted to skip this embarrassing detail in my story, but it'd be foul play. Guess if I'm going to criticize other nations, I should own up to the typical Balkan trickery too.

Transportation strategy – success. We cheerfully cycled back home.

By the way, finding a home had also proved to be quite an intriguing experience in Signland. First, we got a two-story house. It was brand new, listed for sale but they let us live there for a reasonable price until they could secure a deal. A porch, a fireplace, a Jacuzzi … welcome gifts from the land of high standards of living. Too bad we had to move out soon afterwards because a buyer turned up. Or maybe there was no buyer at all. Maybe the neighbors had complained about the few underage jamborees we threw there. After we left, the *FOR SALE* sign remained firmly ensconced on the front lawn.

We needed a new home somewhere close to Seven Corners. The only person who agreed to provide us with a cheap one was Señora Rosario, our new landlady. When it came to accommodation, Rosario was exceptionally helpful. If her basement could be divided into two rooms, she'd find a way to create three living spaces instead and then rent four of them out. She made it clear that we had no business upstairs, but I sneaked in one evening. Plenty of "rooms" there too, separated by bed sheets hung up on wires. Two weeks later I checked again and was relieved to find that she'd made the effort to replace the sheets with plywood. She probably used the money from our rent for that.

Given the number of people that inhabited Señora Rosario's basement, getting the bathroom and hot water to yourself was a challenge indeed. I had to put up with a cold shower after the bike ride, then proceeded to the only mirror available. It hung in the alleged kitchen, a cramped, stomach-turning place. On top of everything, one of the tenants had adopted a kitten and every time I turned on the kitchen light the whole room would start squirming, mostly in the vicinity of the cat bowl. *Hello there, roaches!*

As I was doing my makeup, something rustled in the little space behind the mirror. Now this couldn't be considered a room even by Rosario's standards. It was more of a cupboard. I dearly wanted to believe there were no rats in the basement, but the thought of a living person fitting into the cupboard was inconceivable. I knocked gently. And a living person opened the door.

"Nice clothes," he said sulkily before scurrying up the stairs.

Jamal. Always obsessed with whether your clothes were nice or not. He came from Morocco and initially claimed that he worked for the government here. Highly doubtful. He smelled richly of food so one time I shot him with my suspicion that he worked as a cook. "I cook for the government," Jamal clarified. Apparently he didn't give a damn what he did as long as it was a government job. This immigrant's model must derive from the unmatched pride of every Signlander who happens to work for the government, or has a close relative who does so.

Jamal was always stripped to the waist, wearing nothing but flip-flops and shorts. Yet he never stopped talking about the stash of nice clothes he had. Gel was invariably applied to his curly hair with the utmost diligence, and he bathed in perfume. Jamal acted squeamish too: back when we'd arrived at Rosario's he used to occupy the best room upstairs. He delighted daily in snickering at us for living with The Big Cockroach in the basement. Jamal's particular accent made the cockroach sound even bigger than it actually was.

The circumstances of our little encounter that Friday were obvious. Jamal, not having enough cash to pay the rent for the luxury upstairs, refused to leave. Rosario couldn't call the cops in a house bursting with illegals. Having no way to get rid of Jamal, she decided to accommodate him in the cupboard instead. So here he was, sharing Harry Potter's fate in the very center of The Big Cockroach's premises.

At last we were ready to bounce. Our wish was to settle down at a cozy café and kill an hour or two like we do back home. No luck there. Apparently the place we chose was too busy because the staff kept giving us hints – gentle at first, then not so much – that we weren't expected to overstay their welcome. We had to leave pretty soon.

"What's wrong with you people?" I thundered in the middle of the street.

I was really pissed off. Sure, it's good to keep busy, but it all becomes meaningless if you forget how to rest.

"Money's like toilet paper, you know? Life feels cleaner with it 'cause it sucks to be out of toilet paper. Still, having all the paper in the world isn't gonna necessarily make you happy!"

I roared at random people; the random people stared at me, confused by the mad foreign language I was roaring in.

"Time's well-spent only if you're earning dough, huh? But do you spend the dough well? All you ever do is buy useless appliances and stay home, putting off meaningful experiences for later in life. Think it's better to travel the world when you get Alzheimer's?"

The random people calmed down. Knowing the name of my disease was so reassuring.

"What the fuck, Alice!" Chris hated it when I got too loud. "Can't you stop complaining for one second? First you don't like the signs, you don't like everybody following them, doing their job, the next minute what you don't like is the complete opposite – people in the neighborhood making trouble. What could ever please you, for fuck's sake?"

"Who said I don't like people making trouble? They're like Seven Corners, they remind me of home."

After my outburst was over we decided to at least get a bite to eat. There were a few nice restaurants in the area but they cost an arm and a leg, and part of your torso as well. So it was Mickey D's for us again. We had hamburgers and strawberry shakes. Beaming fair-haired kids loomed from a poster over the only empty booth. The exact slogan escapes me but it implied that Mickey D's was good for your children.

"Let's get out of here!" I said, eyes pinned to the lie.

We took refuge on the swings in a nearby park.

It was a beautiful, sweaty evening. The swings offered a view of the river – beautiful and wet like any other river in the world. The difference here, bearing in mind that we lived near the capital, was that every square meter of space had a person assigned to take care of it. Okay, perhaps not *every* square meter, but it certainly seemed like it. You'd be enjoying the ambience when…

**PLEASE, DO NOT USE THE SWING
FOR MORE THAN 10 MINUTES
SO OTHERS CAN USE IT AS WELL!**

A sign for that too? I jumped off. I didn't feel like swinging or eating anymore. Fed up with the DOs and especially with all the DON'Ts, we left the park in a rush. They were about to lock it up for the night anyway and I didn't want to be kicked out. I'd had enough for one night.

Developed societies are known for always having a Plan. Where we come from, we always have a Plan B. If there's no coffee and chill, then off we go to the clubs.

"Call that guy, the one with the hookers," Chris suggested.

A few days earlier we were thinking about another night out and Jamal had given us the number of one of his buddies. A taxi driver who made "big dough" – he was friends with some pimps and drove their hookers around. This guy allegedly owed a pile of favors to Jamal, so he was supposed to give us a free ride to some fancy club. We'd decided to stay in that night, but "TAXI" was still in my contacts.

He picked up immediately. I could barely make out what he was saying in his strange accent, and he wasn't any luckier with my responses. Jamal was next to him – his constant chatter was audible.

After a few disoriented calls they finally found us. Grinning and flapping his hands about excitedly, like some weird conductor on meth, Jamal had obviously forgotten about our little cupboard episode. We took off. It was a bumpy ride; felt as if we were riding a donkey, and the taxi driver tried to turn us into mules too. There was a good opportunity coming, he said, so was Chris man enough to drive a car full of drugs? A man's payment for a man's job. Chris didn't feel the need to prove his manhood in these particular circumstances, so he declined. Nevertheless, the guy kept on bragging about his criminal ways. We had to listen to one of his more recent exploits, start to finish: he and his "brothers" ordered a pizza to a fake address, then they ambushed the delivery guy in the hall, beat the hell out of him (this part was told in minute detail) and stole his earnings for the day.

By the time we got to the club I had a headache. The taxi driver's sharp, slitty eyes frustrated me further, for they remained glued to me in the rearview mirror. A thin, cheeky smile on his face. He vanished at last, off to his hookers, but Jamal opted to stay with us. Well, things can never be perfect.

This was our first night clubbing in Signland. It didn't feel awkward. When it comes to partying and getting drunk, people around the globe are alike. Jamal insisted that we buy him drinks in return for the free ride. We insisted on buying him *the first* drink and him getting whatever he wanted after that himself. The booze was quite expensive, even though it contained more ice than vodka. Jamal pulled a long face and wandered off somewhere.

It was barely two in the morning, I hadn't even finished my second glass of ice vodka, when the club closed. We found Jamal in front of the entrance.

"You no pay for vodka, we no drive you back!" He was still moody.

Chris adopted a down-to-business expression and shoved his head into Jamal's curl-framed face.

"Now listen, buddy," he hissed. "You and your friend better take us wherever we want to go after telling us all about your little scams on the way here."

I almost choked on a tsunami of laughter. It was hilarious how people here fell for cheap movie lines like this! But they did – the taxi driver came back to pick us up and took us to the lifeguards' party. On the way he offered to show us another club. It was called 5 a.m. and stayed open until morning, he told us.

"Some shady guys go there, there's drugs and…"

"We're good, thank you!" No way in hell was I getting under the same disco ball as individuals who seemed shady even to him.

We arrived at the party at last. Most of the lifeguards had already left because of their curfews. The majority of kids still present were either throwing up or lying unconscious on the consciously trimmed lawn. The booze was in the basement. Those who were fairly sober took us there, eager to demonstrate how the others had fallen into their unpleasant state. They taught us how to play a few drinking games. Same as their parents, kids in Signland aren't aware they can simply chill and enjoy their drinks. That's why they've invented dozens of games to help them get wasted without wasting precious time.

One of the guys, Andrew was his name, really loved our company. "Eastern Europeans" sounded very exciting to him, much like "Russian mafia." We never bothered to explain that we came from a completely different country. Andrew was slightly older than the rest of the lifeguards, but more in age than in brains. Started hitting on me the moment he saw me at the party. Admittedly, he was hot. If he'd had someone to write his pickup lines for him, I might've gone for it. But there was no prompter, so I walked home with Chris. And Boro, of course.

On Saturday morning all of us lifeguards were tainted by the lack of sleep. Boss had us line up as usual. Check-up from head to warts. Shades. Whistle and swimsuit. First-aid kit on the waist… Oops! Andrew had forgotten his kit. The punishment was "twenty push-ups, all of you!" Everyone got to it straight away. Except me. I wasn't good at push-ups and didn't want to embarrass myself. Boss couldn't let me question his authority though.

"Alice, why aren't you down doing push-ups?"

"I'm not your soldier!"

"That was a winning answer. The award: clock out and go home for the day," I say after Annie reads my Signland story.

"But that's so cool! You weren't worried about being fired?"

She is so different from everyone else. No reproachful disbelief in her questions, she never tells me off. The concept of being fired doesn't bother her, not at all. It doesn't seem like a grave life tragedy, and it's not the subject of her sweatiest nightmares. The most likely reason is that Annie doesn't have a job to be fired from and she doesn't have nightmares, for that matter. Still, she has her opinion on such topics and it coincides with the philosophy of my inner voice: people can't see that sometimes leaving their job is exactly what will empower them to go after their dreams.

"Frankly, I didn't think losing my job was even an option. I was pretty sure that when I showed up the next day, Boss would want to have a word with me, and I could easily turn that word in my favor. I'd just say that I'd never been expected to do push-ups in my home country, that I wasn't used to that kind of stuff and his forcing me to do it stank of

DISCRIMINATION. Boss would sweat three times over when I uttered the sinister word. DISCRIMINATION. It wouldn't even dawn on him that my statement had technically no grounds at all."

Annie hurricanes into her typical laughter. PFRRSS-MHOO-MHOO-GHE-KE-KE-CHSHEE-HEE-HEE-HEE. PFRRSS-MHOO-MHOO-GHE-KE-KE-CHSHEE-HEE-HEE-HEE!

"Whenever we had any problems in Signland," I continue after she's finished guffawing her ass off, "the accusation of DISCRIMINATION always did the trick. But it was tricky too, dealing with all those standards of politically correct speech. Looking down from their pedestal of self-righteous individuals who'd never say forbidden words aloud, Signlanders are quick to preach and chastise without realizing that just like with everything else, human efforts to correct their own behavior often lead to outright censorship. Some really non-judgmental folks are forced to constantly watch their mouth, or censor their art, whereas there are so many people out there who speak politically correct, yet judge everyone all the time.

Annie interrupts my train of thought.

"I love your description of Signland. Write some more about Friday nights there."

Down the Hole

My hands trembled. My heart pounded even worse. Blue lights. Another rush of fake politeness. Police politeness while they cuffed my trembling hands, politely stuffed my pounding heart into a patrol car. Next, a fluorescent-lit room jammed with other people's hands in cuffs. Hands of all colors. Trembling and episodic, like a dream, and not a pleasant one.

A Friday night in jail.

Being arrested is the greatest attraction in the land symbolized by the Statue of Liberty. And boy, did I have it coming!

With pool season over, Chris and I decided to indulge in a road trip before leaving the country – half of the East Coast, all the way down to the Magic City. It was a crazy week. I did things I'm not proud of, things I'd never thought of doing in my own country. Maybe because back home they didn't feel so forbidden. All those signs really turned on my inner rebel. I came to understand the miscreant immigrants; all of a sudden it was utterly important to demonstrate that I could do anything I wanted, how no one in the world could stop me. I danced down countless streets, climbed all kinds of fences, skinny-dipped in the ocean (Chris loved that), skinny-dipped in every fountain I came across at night (Chris hated that), and couldn't care less about people watching.

I think there's a special and very mischievous spirit that brings together like-minded people on the road. Throughout our trip we met other rebels who added spice to our journey.

Smooth black guys smoking pot in front of a gas station on our way to an old mansion tour. They stared us down at first, but then offered us some. Chris, stoned as fuck, got bitten by an alligator on the grounds of the mansion. The reptile seemed "very friendly" and he thought it was a brilliant idea to pet it despite the plethora of big signs warning that the alligators might attack if disturbed.

Champagne. Sex on the grass. An illicit sunrise viewed from a park after some Asian kids showed us where to sneak in. Even simple stuff felt like an adventure because someone had bothered to specify it was illegal.

Naturally, the first thing we did when we arrived in the Magic City was go to the famous beach. We couldn't afford any of the restaurants, hotels, art galleries or designer shops, but we could afford the palms and the sand. Chris bought alcohol, plastic cocktail glasses and paper parasols from a cheap store and started mixing tequila sunrises right there on the crowded beach. A typical Chris-thing. He was such a bore most of the time, all serious, wholesome and strict, but every now and then his cool side would show up, and when it did, he was really something.

Chris's bartending caught the attention of a group of gorgeous, well-tanned girls who asked if they could join us. Obviously they needed a break from the usual rich guys because they spent the whole afternoon at our plastic mini-party, dying of laughter, and eventually invited us for a night out. We were filthy because we weren't spending money on hotels during our road trip. Whenever Chris got too tired to drive, he'd park the rental car in the nearest rest area and we'd sleep there. Meaning that, for the last many days, we'd brushed our teeth and hastily washed whatever parts of our bodies we could in rest-area public bathrooms. On the other hand, we couldn't miss nightclubbing in the Magic City. Who'd do that? We showed up for our rendezvous with the girls in our best wrinkled clothes, after having a bath and a shave in a public restroom at the beach. No one cared. Everyone thought we were hilarious and we did our best to dance and chat with people from as many countries as possible. I loved them all. I felt like a part of the world, and the world was cozy and safe. One of the best nights ever.

"So that's what you do. You're a girl who likes getting into fountains and trouble."

"Don't you like getting into fountains and trouble?"

"Sure. That's why I spoke to you in the first place."

And then came shoplifting. It all started with Sister Chelsea.

Movie junkies that Chris and I are, we thought we'd visit some filming locations on our way back from the Magic. It was the climax of our episodes of binge-sneaking behind janitors' backs and fence climbing. We even managed to get into a high school building because of a show we'd watched when we were teenagers. There was a famous cheerleading routine in the show. Upon seeing a group of cheerleaders rehearsing in the real school, I took out my phone to shoot a video. They asked me what I was doing. I explained I was a fan of the show and all of a sudden, everyone became overly enthusiastic about parading in front of the camera. At some point I realized my lousy pronunciation must've had them thinking that I was auditioning them for a new season or something. We hurried out before getting in trouble.

Right afterward, Chris drove to a house we'd seen on the same show. It was locked, but the garage door was open and there she was, bathed in dusty sunlight, ready for the taking: Sister Chelsea, with her big smile, big tits, big everything. An adorable nurse sex doll. It struck me immediately that she'd make the best souvenir to take home from Signland. I didn't think it was stealing – after all, the house didn't seem to belong to a particular person, but to a rich film studio. So off we drove, the big box with Sister Chelsea seated comfortably in our car. I loved the thrill of it.

A couple of towns later, we went to a mall to do some clothes shopping. It was the first time I noticed the signs with the cameras.

SHOPLIFTERS
WILL BE
PROSECUTED

They were everywhere. Before that, I'd never felt like shoplifting, but suddenly I kind of wanted to rise to the challenge. And just like that, for a slinky luxurious belt, a pair of new earrings and a loud beep at the exit of the store that sold them, we were brought in. Chris too because I'd made him carry the luxurious belt for me. I can see now how pathetic it all was. But don't the most adrenaline-packed memories go back exactly to the moments when we do stupid things?

We had exceeded the rule of $100, so they took us straight to the police station.

"Your bail is $1,000, ma'am," a female officer at a desk behind thick glass told me. "Will somebody be coming to pay it for you?"

"I'm not a citizen of the country and I don't know anyone here."

"You'll have to wait in custody until your trial then."

"I have money in my bank account! There must be an ATM here?"

"No, ma'am, there's no ATM here."

"Can't someone escort me to the nearest ATM so I can withdraw the money?"

"No, ma'am, I'm afraid that's not possible."

"Can't *you* just go and withdraw the money for me?"

"No, ma'am, I'm afraid that's not possible. Somebody has to come and pay it for you."

I swallowed my pride and called the Puerto Rican from the pool. He was bound to come to our rescue, he was always so eager to help.

"Sorry, Alice, I don't really want to get involved in this…"

He hung up. Same with Jamal. I went back to the officer behind the thick glass.

"No one's coming for me, but I *have* the money in my bank account. Surely I'm not the first one to be in this situation. What do people usually do?"

"Normally, they call a bail bondsman, but…"

"A bail what?"

"A bail bondsman, ma'am. A person you hire to come and get you out for a certain additional fee. Bail bondsmen don't work with foreigners though."

Pity. I was intrigued to see what someone in this line of work looked like.

"So what should I do then?" I asked in the end.

"Well, ma'am, just stay put and wait until Monday. Your trial will prolly be set for Monday, you being a foreigner an' all. Then you can go."

A cop in the Balkans would never be so polite. Considering I was a first-time offender, they'd just call me "a pain in the ass" and let me go. Anyway, I was far from the Balkans, and I was kindly given the privilege to enjoy an all-inclusive weekend in jail.

They took my mugshot. Profile. Full face. Made me strip down to my thong and gave me some rough pajamas that felt like wearing cardboard. Finally, I was escorted to a cell.

A keycard door. Then a second, and a third one. High ceilings, really high. Long corridors. A fifth keycard door. I hated high ceilings! Seventh door, bars… Long corridors weren't my thing either. Tenth door. There it was, the cell I was supposed to stay in.

Well, my mind didn't stay there for too long. When you're surrounded by narrow ugliness, all you want to do is sleep for eternity. I was down, that is, so down that I spent all day Saturday in Dreamland. There was no reason to wake up. From time to time I heard the sounds of prison around me: my cellmate snoring, then getting up to pee (at least that's what I thought at first), and then the *plop* of something landing in the toilet bowl next to our bunk. She went to eat too. I wanted none of it – no prison food and definitely no plopping it down that toilet. I was fine in Dreamland.

On Sunday I decided I'd better get up. I was incarcerated anyway, why waste the opportunity to look around, meet people, get a feel for the place. A true writer would enjoy every second of it, and that was what I made up my mind to do. I introduced myself to the woman who took a dump with such incredible ease. Kate. She was in for five years already and it wasn't her first time. A serial credit-card scammer.

"But why do you keep doing it if you always end up in prison?"

I'd always been curious about the psychology of re-offenders. Alas, I couldn't get most of Kate's explanation. She didn't speak the same English as me. However, the prevalence of "they's" over "I's" in her story, along with the heavy amount of "God's will" made me conclude that she just didn't want to be in the driver's seat of her life. Maybe jailbirding was her way to deny responsibility. I didn't want to judge though. Kate treated me fine.

"Girl, you're definitely comin' to lunch with me today. You ain't eaten a thing since you got here. You gotta eat!"

I had other worries on my mind.

"It's so cold in here…"

Despite the sticky heat outside the temperature in the prison was terribly low.

"Imagine bein' damn cold for years!" Kate said. "I know what it feels like, but I read the Bible and it warms me righ' up. Out there, I couldn't really un'erstand what the Bible was all about. Now I'm happy that I can read it! I learnt about all the terrible shit that will happen to me if I don't believe… Terrible, terrible shit! But I believe, so I'm saved! You believe in God, Alice?"

"No," I said without hesitation.

"Jesus!" Kate exclaimed. She might've even crossed herself. "I ain't never heard anybody say they didn't believe in God like that! I pity you, girl!"

She pitied me. That was a good one. My mind was instantly flooded with images of the most religious people I'd seen. Ritual killers in movies. Guys wearing crosses at Seven Corners, their eyes ready to sin with me in every possible way. Not for the world would I believe in the same thing they believed in! Besides, I couldn't see why I should honor a particular god if I still managed to hope, love, and do occasional good on my own without divine help. I didn't need the Ten Commandments to realize it's not cool to murder people or covet my neighbor's life. Strict religion is for the insane – they can kill and burn in its name, then confess, repent, and restart with a clean slate.

After lunch (I didn't touch it today either, much to the joy of the others at my table who gladly claimed it) we were allowed half an hour in the fresh air. This meant a small courtyard with mesh on the top and a tiny piece of sky above the mesh. One of the girls asked me why I was in jail. My eyes started to water.

"We don't cry in here," a cruel-looking inmate shouted, but the others gathered around to console me.

"Oh, shoplifting's nothing. We do it all the time."

"You tried to steal from Macy's? Everyone knows Macy's no place for stealin'."

After dinner it was shower time. All the girls fiercely protected their place in line in front of the curtained alcove with the shower. The curtain didn't fall all the way down to the floor so the wardens could see the feet of the inmate inside. I had zero desire whatsoever to try skipping the line and irritating any Amazons, so I waited humbly in the back, cradling the rag they gave us for a towel. I must've looked miserable as hell, because the Amazon who was first in line, the cruel-looking one from the courtyard, let me go in her place. All the girls I'd talked to gave us a look of approval: the DUI inmate who called her boyfriend every day from the prison payphone, hoping he'd wait for her faithfully out there; the 18-year-old who'd pushed drugs at her school, who'd told me she was no lesbian or anything but she thought I was beautiful; Kate with her motherly concern. I had my official opinion now: women in jail weren't that bad, no matter what signs their fellow countrymen labeled them with. Women in jail weren't judgmental.

Before we went to bed, Kate asked me to fix her hair, still damp after the shower, into petite braids.

"So I look all curly and nice at the hearin' tomorrow," she said.

She sang while I was braiding, hopeful and excited, as if she were getting ready for a job interview. She seemed a bit frightened too, maybe more from the prospect of real life than from the one of staying in prison. She had everything here: a bed with her Bible under the pillow, a full course of meals to keep her entertained from dawn to dusk, and reasons to braid her hair. I imagined Kate getting her hair fixed for her interview with God someday.

Monday.

They drove us to court with our hands *and* ankles cuffed. I felt like a real hard-boiled criminal. An hour later, they let me go with a two-month probation period.

I took the bus to the city, stealing suspicious glances at my fellow passengers. They'd got on with me at the stop in front of the prison, after all, who knew what they were up to.

They too looked at me with suspicion. My shabby appearance made it clear where I'd come from.

I called my mom from a payphone.

As I dialed I remembered my dad shouting when I'd called them from the police station two days before.

"You idiot! I'll kick your ass when you get home!"

I could almost feel his angry spit through the receiver. My dad shouts a lot, but he also has this great sense of dark humor. I knew he'd see the comic side of things by the time I got back.

After giving me a proper slap on the wrist, he'd put my mom on the phone.

"Shoplifting?! Alice, how could you do something like that? Where are you now? You're fine, right? Beg them to let you go. I'll call to beg them too... And by no means talk back to the police, you hear me? Don't you dare!"

That's my mother for you. Always the polite, kind, respectable woman. Forever concerned that we'd make fools of ourselves in front of others, making a fool of yourself meaning, variously, getting ice-cream stains on your shorts, laughing too loudly, or speaking the truth about our dysfunctional family. It didn't suit her having a daughter like me, one that never failed to end up in trouble. But I got this from the Bohemian rebel of a man she chose to marry. She had to put up with me. Overwhelmed by my actions, she'd nag me, then help me out, then nag some more, then help and help and help again...

This time when she picked up, I told her about the outcome of the trial and she couldn't even find it in her heart to scold me too hard. All she wanted was for me to come back home in one piece. I felt bad about what I'd done to her with my little prison adventure, but I didn't know how to apologize. So I moved on to my wish list:

"Mom, promise you'll cook for me when I get back home! I want chicken soup. And meatballs with tomato sauce, and pork with rice, and stuffed peppers too! My plane lands at 12. No, no, no need for you to come to the airport. Chris' father will pick us up."

I seriously intended to eat all that for lunch. I lied about our time of arrival though. Chris and I were supposed to land at 11, but we'd decided to have one last coffee together before going home.

A few days later, on the plane, Sister Chelsea safely nested at my feet, I looked down at the clouds. I remembered how terrified my sister had been a couple of months earlier when I'd told her I was flying away to Signland: "I'm afraid to think of you getting on that plane! What if something awful happens?!"

I'd laughed her worries away: "No biggie! Worst case I'll have a brand new story about surviving a plane crash!"

We were so different, my sis and I. Textbook cases of a pessimist and an optimist. However, she had also gotten on a plane in the meantime. I thought she'd panic. Not in the least. She'd texted me that she didn't have time for the slightest bit of anxiety. No one had ever told her how beautiful it was to look at the world from above.

It's as simple as that. Beauty is more powerful than pessimism or optimism. I learned to truly appreciate that in prison; picked it up from the inmates. It may sound strange, but their aspiration for beauty was more contagious than anything else I'd ever witnessed. Almost all of the female inmates drew, mostly flowers. I didn't have the chance to observe the men much – I was in the women's ward after all – but as I was strolling toward the exit, already free, a male inmate in an orange jumpsuit and cuffs passed by me.

"Good for you, sweetheart!" he cheered. "Off you go! This is no place for a beautiful kid like you."

And he meant it, no envy, no dirty hints.

"You don't belong in here!"

"I don't belong
out there either!"

"So did you enjoy Signland or not?" asks Annie as she puts my jail story down.

"Big time! I always love an adventure, even if it's shitty at times. Especially if it's shitty at times."

Annie nods with pleasure. I'm encouraged to launch into one of those loquacious monologues she always inspires in me. Ardent monologues. Larger than life.

"You know what? I wasn't even prejudiced before I went there. I thought stereotypes were bullshit. I thought people were the same everywhere. But then I saw for myself. Even if we're all born the same, our environment is a great influence too. With Signlanders, you never know if someone has their own strong sense of morality, or they're simply obeying the rules.

"I didn't go to see any monuments of the past. Who cares about the expressionless faces of statues turned toward a stone future that will never exist? You get to learn so much more by gazing into the eyes of the living people around. And Signlanders' eyes… They seem to have lost their keenness, for the most part. Only the smiles of the jack-o'-lanterns are still there. Wider than the Cheshire Cat's smile. Whiter than the White Rabbit. Pumpkin smiles all over the place!

"I didn't go to see the Statue of Liberty because I didn't see any liberty. A police state of freedom? They must be kidding. In a truly free land, Anarchy and Harmony would be able to get along well. Street dogs can do this, you know. No restrictions for them, no rules, and they seem so much more relaxed than our pet dogs. We humans are simply bound to screw everything up. No rules, and we go crazy. Too many rules, and we go fucking insane. Perhaps all political ideologies are good in the beginning but we just can't let them work out for the best. Disorder after socialism here, the all-consuming consequences of capitalism there, destruction after every single –ism we've ever invented. How come everybody realizes that the golden middle is the perfect state of existence, yet we always go to extremes? This question won't bring me peace, and then I just go to extremes too.

"Anyway, I had my ups and downs in Signland, but I don't regret any of it. Every country, every town, every neighborhood is a whole different world worth exploring. Every journey makes life longer. A month of being stuck in the same spot, doing the same things over and over again, is an entirely different sensation than a month of visiting different places. You'd think the traveling month would fly by quickly, but in your memories, it will remain as a long-lasting life experience."

"Sweet!" A cheeky sparkle in Annie's eyes. "But you don't even have to travel physically in order to explore different worlds. Every new hobby is a new world. Every new job. Exploring a religion. Every time you fall in love, the city you thought you knew so well becomes a completely different place. Every new friendship reveals more about people. Same with every new enemy. If you get paranoid about something, the world will change once again because you'll see it all in the light of fear... So what happened after Signland? Write about Alice's adventures in other lands too... Like Lewis Carroll."

"But I'm not even that into Lewis Carroll's tales about Alice."

"Try your own version."

There's hardly enough space for me in my bed as it is. Sheets upon sheets upon sheets of written paper. But I keep going. I write and write. I don't edit. I'm still in awe of this new razor-sharpness in my mind. Annie waltzes around.

The Looking Glass

Jail wasn't a big deal. In Signland, I managed to fall in love too – now that was what broke all hell loose.

The usual story. A girl from the Balkans goes to work and travel across the ocean and loses her mind over some cute foreigner there. His name was Jack. A trivial name to match a trivial situation. He worked with us at the pool and he was thunderstruck – as he admitted to me later – by my denial to do push-ups for Boss. Soon after that it was my turn to be thunderstruck. Jack's wording of love left me wordless. Exquisite gestures of adoration as well. After the fair share of douchebags I'd dated before, he was a sanctuary.

You know the kind of love that burns you down to ashes, which is so complex that when your lover holds you tight after a gruesome fight, you catch yourself thinking you'd die happily right there and then should the world collapse on top of your head at that very moment? Well, there was no burning down to ashes with Jack. We didn't fight, and whenever he held me tight all I knew was he'd never let the world harm me in any possible way. What else can I say about heavenly love? You can't be bothered to write about it. Your only desire is to experience it to the max. Art is more about bleeding, I guess, not so much about depicting pure feelings of happiness. With heavenly love, there are only sunny days and candle-lit evenings; no mountains to climb, no oceans to drown in, no hearts to be conquered. They readily surrender from the very beginning. And if they're bound to part for some reason, heavenly love will endure to remind us that it did somehow exist, even if only for a brief moment in time.

Jack couldn't join us on our eventful road trip. I never told him that his goddess had ended up behind bars. Sometimes angels and demons are entitled to share the same heavenly love. Poor demons. There's nothing we can do but cover up our bad deeds, then we feel guilty about lying.

In the little time we actually spent together, our bodies trembled with love every second. After I left, we made the mistake of transferring this trembling to our fingers, hovering over keyboards in two, too far away countries.

Alice_in_Love: Miss you, Jack :(
Jack O'Love: I love u so fuckin much babe!!!

Six months of lame texting. Then Jack did the lamest thing ever: he bailed and blocked me everywhere, saying that he wished to be with me "forever, but forever doesn't start now." I could see his mom's pursed lips behind this decision. She was convinced that the only reason I was interested in her son was a green card. It never occurred to her that maybe not everyone was obsessed with the idea of moving to the realm of signs.

My devotion for Jack took its time to auto shut down. It's hardly true that out of sight means out of mind. More often than not, out of sight means steadfast idealization. Heavenly love makes you feel like a child. As happy as a child on a butterfly-filled meadow at first. As lost as a child in the woods when it's taken from you.

I tried to replace my Jack with Jack Daniel's. A proven recipe for getting over hurt feelings that dated back to my teenage years: tons of aimless partying and liters of booze. Eventually, I got sick of both. I was also sick of my friends constantly saying "I told you so!" Even before Jack stopped texting, my nearest and dearest were already bitching about how long-distance relationships were always doomed. There's nothing wrong with the distance – less than 10,000 km, which is 38.4 times less than the distance to the moon. And as far as I know, Man has landed on the moon. No distance is doomed, people are. It was the difference between mindsets – mine, Jack's, and his family's – that was doomed. A difference as substantial as the gap between a human mindset and that of an overdeveloped plankton living in the postmodern environment of a faraway planet. Signlanders like to wrap all their optimistic romance into Hollywood movies so they won't need to fight for it in real life. That's what I think. It sucked that I couldn't just go to Target and ask for a refund. *This love is kaput! I want my tears back right now!*

"Why do you love me, Jack?"
"Because you're so deep. But you also scare me, babe."
"Haha, I do? Why?"
"You're too deep."

I couldn't stop daydreaming about him. My friends spent the entire summer dragging me from one bar to another. So I could forget, they said. "I told you so! I told you so!" Their mantra haunted me, mixed up with the rhythm of house music from the clubs. *Untz-untz! Tol-toldya!* The beat made me dizzy and I'd escape to the bathroom with my beautiful thoughts about Jack. My chance to shed a tear for him without being scolded.

Sometimes a bathroom is the only matchbox where you can be alone with your thoughts.

Suddenly, being alone felt utterly appealing. I stopped asking people over for parties. Didn't attend theirs. No more waking up to huge bags of garbage and hungover bodies spread across the living room floor. I no longer went to classes. Even quit my job teaching English that I'd found after I came back from Signland. I wanted to stay home. I didn't want to see anyone.

"Let's watch porn the next time we have sex." Me, coming up with spicy ideas. I'd heard men loved this.

"All right, if it's a turn-on for you."

Jack didn't look at the TV once. That blaze in his pupils was completely focused on me.

Who'd have thought the Nice Guy could hurt you so bad?

It was all my fault though. My inner climate shouldn't have been dependent on someone's winds and whims of emotion. Nor on their actions. If you're not happy on your own, you can't be happy with anyone else. In the big game of existence, it was time for me to level up to the Life on My Own section, dedicating my Friday nights to the DIY club, rather than to getting wasted with friends.

In the DIY club, you don't depend on anyone.

A do-it-yourself light bulb: it turns on inside you when darkness falls.

A do-it-yourself switch for the bulb.

A heater for the heart: you won't freeze in other people's cold anymore.

Learn how to cook for one: sauce to your own liking.

"Mirror, mirror on the wall, who's the fairest of them all?" I asked.

The answer was lengthy and bleak:

"The fairest of them all is Alice who lives in a room. Eyes red as blood. Lips white as snow. Hair that has lost its luster for any particular color. Nobody locked Alice in her room. Fearful Winter roams across the city and Alice doesn't feel like going out in the cold. She doesn't feel like working. She doesn't feel like meeting people. She doesn't feel like doing anything they expect her to do. She sleeps all day long, and there's not a single dwarf in her bed. Only Insomnia comes to visit at night.

"Alice doesn't care to bathe either. Ball gowns hang in the wardrobe forgotten, and by the stains on her bathrobe, one can tell what she's been eating for the past week. She dines on whatever she can find; her cage is strewn with empty plates, unwashed glasses, sticky wrappers of snacks sweet and salty. The only thing Alice doesn't ingest are apples. She never liked them for some reason.

"Dinner together has never been a thing in Alice's family. They aren't on the same schedule; they don't live the same life. Alice's mother, a morning person, comes home tired from work and likes to dine early. Her father stays up late. He likes to drink. Before meeting what she imagined to be her Prince Charming, Alice was fine with all that. But then Jack spoiled everything. "I want to have babies with you and we'll all have dinner together every night at 7 o'clock. That's what happy families do." Jack always dined with his parents. The void between the vision he created and the reality of Alice's dim-lit room is heartbreaking.

"Time doesn't matter when you are locked in a room. Alice replaces the *tick-tock* of the clock with the *click-click* of her mouse and the *husk-husk* of cracking sunflower seeds. When sitting around with nothing to do, sunflower seeds are crucial. And *husk-husk* would make a great soundtrack for a thriller about a ghost of a girl who suffers from depression."

Yup. The mirror on the wall gave me a precise answer. I was 23, a year had passed since I'd come back from Signland, and I was serving a sentence of depression at home.

Winter depression. It started in October or November, the most hateful months. Days growing shorter and shorter. Mornings pissed on by the sad rain. Prematurely born evenings in incubators. Lousy months when only winter-sports fans and suckers for Christmas can buy the lie that something nice is approaching. I've never understood people who boast that fall is their favorite season. "But it's so beautiful!" Perverse trees stripping down until they turn into striptease poles. Some breathtaking aesthetics, no doubt about that!

As an optimist, I'd dealt with fall without much trouble before. This time, however, my optimism was already lying in a heap on the floor after the man of the year openly assaulted it. I didn't feel like surveying the fainting of tree leaves on the streets. My stay-at-home escapism was rather convenient. No one bothered me with their crap there. Every day felt like Sunday, minus the obligation to do things on Monday. I'd only go out for a couple of minutes when I needed to get Boro. Then we'd snuggle together in the privacy of my den.

I didn't need anyone else. Didn't even need Jack anymore. If you're trying to forget something, you must first forget that you're trying to forget it. That's what psychologists say. The easiest way to not remember a number or an appointment is to write it down. And that's exactly how I forgot about Jack. I didn't force it, just rid myself of any reason to think about him. I didn't analyze our breakup with friends anymore. Didn't whine about it. There was no one to discourage me, no one to encourage me, fucking no one to offer me comfort.

I was alone, yet I didn't feel lonely. People are lonely when they're not alone in their thoughts. Disappointed with everyone, my mind was a peaceful place to be.

I still lived with my parents, but they didn't bother me, nor were they bothered by the fact that I barely left my room anymore. I couldn't get into trouble there, I guess. So the only thing that still bugged me was my cell phone. How could my home possibly be my castle if there was a phone constantly shrilling for my attention? The convulsions with which it bore text messages kept gnawing at my silence.

    where r u?

    let's go out for a drink!!!

    miss u ☺

First I stopped replying. Then I stopped reading. One day my phone died with a beep, and I simply didn't recharge it. I was proud to be a person who'd silenced their phone. No one came to ring the doorbell either. The friends who thought they knew me never expected to find me at home.

I declined all invitations for Students' Day. "I have plans already," I said. My plan was to not celebrate. Last year I'd done the same but for different reasons – back then Jack and I were still texting and I couldn't bear to miss our declarations of love even for a night. When a girl in good health, who normally has a strong inclination to party, stays in alone on a Friday night (or even worse, on Students' Day, which is a pretty big deal here), it's clear what's going on: she either has a long-distance relationship, or she's suffering from depression.

I stayed in on New Year's Eve too. It was peaceful. A small depression played with its dolls in my head. Nothing to fuss about, right?

I didn't think I had a serious problem, and Google supported my stance. It informed me that depression was characterized by feelings of inferiority or guilt, suicidal thoughts, and an unwillingness to live. I simply didn't want any people in my life – without them I was doing just great. I felt perfect. Inferiority my ass. I decided that the rest of the world obviously didn't deserve a sunshine like me, so I'd rather give all my attention to myself. Only fools need the human circus to save them from boredom. I awakened my long-forgotten habit of reading, watched movies from a variety of genres and time periods, and listened to music I'd never heard before. I never got bored. The stuff I learned was way more fascinating than what they taught at university.

Once you stop dealing with other people's imperfections, you finally have time to refine your own excellence.

You find the time to write, too. Up until that moment, I'd been too consumed with living. My depression was like a break from life, a break where I had the luxury of free time.

So I wrote. Haphazard pieces. Not particularly long.

I felt beautiful as well as harmonious, regardless of my neglected looks. The most important souvenirs you bring back from a journey to a new world are not the fridge magnets, or even a sex doll, but the new ways of thinking that have been kindled. The dearest souvenir I brought back from Signland was my own beauty. There, strangers of all ages and sexes would stop me on the street to tell me how gorgeous I was. All of my other assets seemed questionable, problematic or too deep. My beauty, however, could enjoy a peaceful cup of coffee at all times. I'd brought this spineless, yet very convenient self-confidence back with me in my suitcase.

The old me would have been offended. It would have stigmatized beauty for being shallow. But I'd grown fond of it. I respected it now. Beauty inhabits its own world and it's always around us. You can go and look for help there when everything else is a mess. Plus, the old me didn't have much say anymore. As a kid and later on as a teenager, I'd received lots of compliments on my intelligence. Every time I felt rejected or different, I could comfort myself by just thinking how smart I was. However, after you've been arrested for shoplifting and dumped by yet another lousy boyfriend, after you've chosen depression over university, people no longer exactly crowd in line to tell you how clever you are. I needed a new source of self-affirmation.

I even refused to celebrate my birthday. It's also in the middle of winter. As if Christmas Eve, Christmas and New Year weren't enough amidst my depression; I could forego the shitty cosmic biorhythm that happens before birthdays on top of all that. For a while now I'd developed a dislike for holidays. They'd lost the spirit they once had, and yet you still felt obliged to act groovy. The fear that you might fail just depressed you further. But a good mood is supposed to be built from the inside out, not to be pinned down on a calendar date. I've seen nights much more entertaining than holiday nights, and flowers much more significant than those given on special occasions.

I still thought it'd be decent to at least have a shower for my birthday. As I was scrubbing myself with the washcloth, I discovered two big spots on the back of my thighs. Strange spots, slightly different in color than the rest of my body, with a distinctive shape – as if I'd held a hot iron to my skin. I was confused for a moment and then it dawned on me. Those were the marks of my permanent posture for the last few months – sitting down cross-legged on the chair before my computer and books. The next day the spots were still there. Same thing the day after. I must admit this side effect of my depression gave me the creeps for a while.

Then I chose to pretend I hadn't noticed the spots.

"Oh, Alice, you're far too obsessive about everything, including being alone. Can't you see? You humans are far too obsessive. If you get overly fixated on taking care of a fish tank, even that will start feeling dramatic. You need to distribute your energy in different directions. That way even if you lose one of them, you won't be completely lost."

"I know. But that's just how I was back then. Every time I fell in love, it would rule my whole world. And given my previous misfortunes, what happened with Jack was too much to bear."

"Maybe it's about time you wrote about those misfortunes."

By this point, I already know what Annie is doing. She's trying to get me to write an entire book.

"*Alice in Loveland…* How about that?" she offers.

"No way. There's no way I'm writing a book about love!"

"All books are about love, Alice."

Alice in Love Chains

„Wanna play husband-and-wife?"

Forever ago, on the playground of my day care center.

"Wanna play husband-and-wife?" one of the boys asked me. The opening line to all circuses gone bad.

I agreed, my right foot shyly poking the sand in the sandbox. This was the beginning of my harsh experience with men. I still recall my young suitor's name – Tommy. I also remember a flutter under my belly button whenever little Tommy would touch me. It was a funny feeling; not that we touched so much, or that we touched in *those* places. We were much less into it than kids are now. These days, at the sight of two firebugs stuck together kids start shouting: "Look! Look! They're having sex, little perverts!" Back then, we used to think that mating firebugs were Siamese twins, and that was fun enough for us too.

The morning we played husband-and-wife there were lots of firebugs on the playground. We pushed them around with sticks for a while. Then we cooked our family lunch of tree-leaf salad and mud meatballs. Dessert was some delicious strawberry toothpaste that we stole from the bathroom. Then we went to our respective beds.

In the afternoon I saw my guy playing husband-and-wife with another girl. I recall her name too – Lora.

I felt so low that day. I don't remember the exact thoughts that came to my naive 4-year-old mind but looking back, I think I should've seen the basic rule already:

Humans are not monogamous. Neither are animals. Some birds are believed to be faithful to a single partner for life, but there are exceptions even among them – I did my research. It turns out that absolute, impeccable, unquestionable monogamy exists only with the parasitic flatworm Diplozoon paradoxum, *a creature that lives on the gills of a particular species of fish. In Asia. And Europe. Those poor little parasites don't have much choice, do they? If they don't meet a partner, they die. And when they do meet a partner, their bodies are fused together right on the first date to remain so till death do them part, unable to cheat even if they dearly wanted to.*

No other species is a hundred percent monogamous. Unlike us, however, other species aren't eternally tormented by their polygamy. They don't bother coming up with questionable romantic morals. They don't make a fuss. This is the huge divergence between humans and animals: ANIMALS DON'T MAKE A FUSS. They don't accuse themselves or their partner of infidelity. The concept of infidelity is unknown to them because they were never stupid enough to invent it. Animals are polygamous because Mother Nature has made them that way, and She is wise and knows best. Mother Nature doesn't waste time – even though She has all the time in the world – to coin abstract terms and then wonder what they mean for the rest of Her life. Words like Love. Infidelity. Goodness.

All other species have an instinct for self-preservation. Humans sport another, unique instinct.

Self-destruction.

Isn't it weird that mankind's favorite plant is a flower with thorns?

We are all unfaithful at some point – if not physically, then at least in our thoughts. Even if just a little, just this once, just because. Many feel guilty about the sinful act too. Or choose to conveniently blame it on their partner. Nature has given us life, and we waste quite a big portion of it suffering because of love. We bear this cross with such pride! And the idea of bearing a cross is yet another ridiculous concept that only the long-suffering Homo sapiens *could come up with.*

In trying to be faithful to one another we are actually unfaithful to Nature. We squirm in a painful attempt to be "virtuous" when we could just squirm with pleasure instead.

Of course, the little girl who ate toothpaste before naptime couldn't fathom such things. Most people spend a lifetime fighting the notion of polygamy. My problem was that I merely acknowledged it in my mind. My heart couldn't take it and made bitter attempts to find pure love for years. I was self-destructive. I destroyed lots of things that didn't belong to me, too.

But before I start with the full-scale drama, let me go back to my platonic thrills.

In first grade I wrote a love letter to a boy who sat next to me in my class. I desperately wanted the letter to be perfect, just like the love I thought I felt at the time, but I couldn't draw a nice heart. So I asked a friend to draw it for me.

The following day the addressee's grandmother stormed into our school waving about my letter and my friend's masterpiece of a heart. She complained to the teacher that I was harassing her grandson. That's how in first grade I learned my second lesson:

As for that grandmother, I never understood what fazed her so much in my letter. Back then I was a pristine, innocent girl. I owned a white ballerina dress and imagined myself getting married to my deskmate in it.

Only a year later did I learn about sex.

One day, I took *Treasure Island* down from the bookshelf at home for the umpteenth time, and guess what! There was a hardcore issue of *Hustler* stashed between the pages. I hid my discovery in another book, and then it was my mom's turn to accidentally find it. In the investigation that followed, my father testified that the troublesome read belonged to a friend of his. The same old trick. Just a year ago, I'd said a friend of mine wrote that love letter to my deskmate.

Before the *Hustler* was confiscated, however, I managed to show it to the other kids on the block. We examined the imagery and the accompanying text in gross detail. A bit earlier *Treasure Island* had inspired me to hide under a blanket in the cabin of my pirate ship where I felt cozy and warm as I traversed new lands and blood-chilling storms. The porn mag also inspired the explorer in us. We built a blanket shelter again, only this time it served a different purpose – to keep us safe from prying parental eyes as the girl from the third floor and the boy next door showed us their lower anatomy.

Once again, trouble came the very next morning. Someone rang our doorbell to death while banging on the door too. It turned out that the girl from the third floor sat in front of the fireplace with her mom every evening to tell her about her day. Her accounts were quite detailed, judging by the state of my behind after her mother had finished spanking me with her slipper. After swearing at me plenty, she moved on to the other young culprits.

Another rule was fleshed out:

If you get involved in even a mere anatomy lesson with people who spend their evenings with mom by the fire, the very least you'll get is a good spanking with a slipper.

By the way, not long afterwards, the girl from the third floor became the nympho on the block. I guess she liked what she saw in the mag more than I did. For many years after that I was pretty confident I'd never do the stuff I saw on those pages; it seemed so messy and gross. Even at the thought of French kissing, most of us kids were quite firm that we'd never get involved in such yucky business. Then one by one everybody started making out and all of a sudden we found ourselves eager to try the yucky stuff too. We even practiced on ice cubes. We clumsily explored the sexual field in all kinds of ways:

Calling phone sex lines – parents printing the call history and shouting at us about the huge phone bill and the nature of the numbers dialed.

Buying condoms – filling them with water and throwing the bombs at passersby from our balconies, then listening to the angry shouts that followed.

Skipping class – trips to the famous sex shop downtown and a good scolding about getting on the tram without permission.

Biology class, page 199, The Reproductive System – the teacher young and quite pretty, the boys gaping at her sophisticated explanations of procreation, the girls already into their acne-driven moodiness, rolling their eyes, a touch jealous of the teacher's smooth sex appeal. "Oh come on, Miss, why so tedious? We've done frog dissection, remember? You can be more open about screwing!" Maria, the class clown.

A late winter afternoon, already dark out, waiting alone at a bus stop – a middle-aged creep approaching me. "Can I just watch you, young lady?" "Yeah, sure…" Crazy or not, it felt like the safest reply. His dick was already out, his hand moving ever more frantically. Done in thirty seconds. Tops. "Thank you so much, young lady!" Then he was gone. I didn't dare look out of more than a corner of my eye but I thought I could smell something sticky and weird in the air. It was amusing how he'd appreciated my willingness to cooperate. He was disgusting, but I wasn't an easy scare and on my part, I appreciated that my diary entry for the day was going to contain something juicy. I didn't tell my parents, of course. Why bother, they wouldn't explain anything anyway; they'd only find something to punish me for.

Grown-ups were always so touchy when kids tried to find out about sex.

And what happened when we teenagers took a practical interest in the matter? We were intimidated: worried that we'd stay virgins until death, afraid that it'd hurt when we did get to lose our virginity, or that we wouldn't know what to do and it'd all be too awkward… Eventually we got the job done. We went to a party. A few tequilas later, it started. A few drops of blood later, it ended. And that was it. Why all the fuss? Why did grown-ups sweat so much that one day we'd start having sex, instead of worrying that one day we'd fall in love?

Sex is much safer than love.
Sex only hurts the first time. Love hurts every time.

Sure enough. When it comes to pain, love can be extremely resourceful. It never fails to surprise you with something that you never thought people were capable of. Or worse, with something you never thought *you* were capable of.

When we're young we all share a similarly chaste attitude toward love and sexual behavior. I doubt any kids imagine themselves cheating one day. Or forgiving their partner's cheating. Forgiving other humiliations as well. Telling lies. Having jealous fights. Being physically aggressive at least once. Crying. Begging. Falling in love with a criminal, sleeping with someone else's lover, threatening to kill themselves, falling for suicidal threats… No. You tuck all that safely under the blanket of the *I'd never…* list.

And then, one day, it all happens to you.

There's a good chance that by the time you're halfway through university only a few things still seem repulsive. Dozens of *I'd never…* have turned into *It just happened….* And were then repeated, a second time, a third time, oh who cares to count. Quite like getting wasted on tequila: almost everyone has a tequila-related story that ends with puking and *Never again!* And almost everyone has a sequel to that story.

In the end, you have no shame left. No fig leaf over your genitals.

"Have you been drinking again?" my mother hissed at my dad.

"Can't you just say 'thanks for the flowers, darling'? I bought the whole fucking shop for you! I'm trying hard here!"

It was her birthday and for the past fifteen minutes a neighbor and I had been watching my dad and his drunk friend carry buckets of flowers up the stairs to Mom. I wished the earth would swallow my blushing soul up. Like right there and then.

"But that's so sweet! Your old man's so romantic!" our neighbor said. "How I wish I could have this kind of Great Love too!"

Yeah, right, the romance in our household! I chose not to tell her how my mom's encyclopedias, as well as her childhood coin and stamp collections, had vanished a week ago only to reappear in the pawn shop. I didn't know how my dad thought getting in debt at the florists too was a good way to apologize.

If that's what Great Love looks like, I don't want any of it.

My own first Great Love occurred soon afterward.

We were in high school. Steve was a bad boy. He was also a very good friend. He didn't speak much, thus allowing me to find whatever I needed in his green eyes, then turn it into poetry. I sucked at poetry but who cared? My mind played out romantic scenarios for hours: on the bus, at the supermarket, at the skating rink, everywhere. The tornado of feelings made me doubt myself all the time. *He loves me, he loves me not!* For days my brain would pluck imaginary petals off imaginary daisies. Why can't we just smile blissfully and enjoy our own feelings? Why are they never enough? Why do we insist on knowing what we're getting in return? Probably because we love ourselves above all else.

"Am I your first kiss?"

"Are you crazy? I've kissed lots of guys before."

He tasted like Orbit Winterfresh. To this day, I always opt for Orbit Winterfresh because it evokes the sweetness of my first kiss.

"You coming to the party tonight?"

"Do you want me to come, Alice?"

"Why would I care? I'm only asking."

I was dying for the opportunity to dance with him, but didn't know if I was supposed to just say so or beg on my knees or what. Pretending I didn't care seemed mature enough. He came nevertheless.

"Hey, I'm here…"

"Great! Is this your friend? He's pretty cute!"

Prom night. He was with a date, but somehow I wound up in his arms.

"You know, for all these years, you've always felt like the only close person I've had. I think I love you, Alice!"

Alice was too drunk to reply.

> Hey, Steve, how're you doing? How's uni? I just
> thought I'd let you know that not seeing you
> every day feels like shit. I didn't realize that was
> what made every week in high school so special. I
> think I've been in love with you all along.

Seen. He didn't text back. The taste of my own medicine wasn't so great.

I can't even say for sure that my love was unrequited. We didn't know how to put things into words, and we had no idea that some things are better done without speaking about them. The whole story remained unfinished, the worst outcome ever. I still dream about him. No, not nightmares; these are the most gentle of dreams, and that's what makes them so sad. When you wake up from a nightmare, relief bursts out with the sweat on your forehead. But when you open your eyes after a happy dream, all you feel is emptiness, as if something precious has been torn from you.

Meanwhile I'd gone through my first-ever "steady" relationship too. It started at the end of my junior year of high school. I was all in from the very beginning. He – not so much. We went to the coast together. One night, after discovering that sex on the beach was probably the most overrated thing ever, we lay on the sand and watched the stars. One fell from the sky.

"What did you wish for?"
"That you'd finally fall in love with me. You?"
"That you'd finally give me a blowjob."
Both wishes came true.

A year and a half later I cheated on him. That's how I found out that screwing things up wasn't a male privilege. I did quite well too. I admitted my infidelity – not because I'd invested much feeling into it; I just wanted us to break up. I wanted to experience more, much more of those crazy, shameful, unforgettable things that happen to single girls. I still thought about my first Great Love too. Was it even possible to truly love someone else?

High-school love is easy. You may be convinced that what you feel is for real, but there aren't too many layers to it. You may cry rivers of teenage tears, yet there will come a day when the memories of those juvenile heartbreaks will only amuse you. It's not likely that they'll scar you for life. More often than not, things get really rough after high school. It's not about how to tell a guy that you like him anymore, or having to explain that you have a curfew. At long last, no one else has any say over what you can and can't do. You're the one who gets to set the limits, or at least you're entitled to choose who gets to set them for you. Your mighty instinct for self-destruction, hand in hand with your unfailing instinct to surpass your own limits, are having the time of their lives, making you constantly play leapfrog with your own values. That's how you find out what it really means to ache.

I met my second Great Love in the beginning of my sophomore year of university. This time it felt more real because I dove in headlong, and when our relationship reached the bottom, not a single romantic image remained of what could have been.

My Love left his car unlocked. He missed business meetings whenever he felt like having a siesta. Charmingly arrogant and self-focused, he boasted that he never told lies because he'd rather hurt his partner with the truth than burden himself with the necessity of remembering untruths. My Love ruled a company of his own and a world of his own, and his manner of entitlement allowed him to steer this world in whatever direction he liked. My Love could show me an abundance of things I hadn't seen yet. So I fell for him, terribly.

His name was George. He was much older than me, divorced, and came with a kid. He came with a girlfriend as well. They'd been together for several years. He claimed they'd split up but it seemed neither of them was really sure about it. She despised me, and he wasn't able to ignore her hysterical fits. She kept calling in the wee hours with the announcements that she was going to kill herself, over and over again. Oh, how I loved that – little suicidal intentions. Still, the first few times I urged him to go and check on her. He went. Then he went again. And again. Comforting the serial suicidal wannabe. She kept calling. And calling. And calling… I still get the creeps when I hear the old iPhone ringtone.

"I love the smell of napalm in the morning!" Colonel Kilgore said in *Apocalypse Now*.
"I love the smell of coffee in the morning!" George would always say.

He taught me that planet Earth was inhabited by men who could easily be with a woman simply because she made coffee for them in the morning; because she was a good housewife, the perfect backup when Mom wasn't around. They didn't need to actually love this living, breathing coffee machine.

"Ah, Alice, you need to understand one thing: women are like appliances. You can always shoot a good video with your iPhone, but if you want a really professional movie, you need to get a cinema camera. Specialized gadgets work on a different level, and it's the same with women. There's simply no chick who can be good in bed *and* in the kitchen. Who can be gorgeous, faithful, and smart at the same time. Or be interested in the things I find intriguing but know about fabric softeners too… It's a myth! There are women that you keep at home, and women that you keep as lovers. You're not fit to be kept at home. But you're still young and don't know anything about these things!"

"I'm not making you any goddamn coffee! I don't want you to be with me just because I make COFFEE!"

"You need to change if you want me to respect you."
"If I change, *I* won't respect myself. I'd rather respect myself than try to impress you."

"Can I shave you? It's a fetish I have."
"I'm shy."
"Ah, Alice, you need to grow up!"
"Fine. Are we using your razor?"
No fig leaf over your genitals. The fig leaf is covering your heart now.

Before I crashed into my relationship with George, I had the psychological resilience of a child. I firmly believed in love. He and his dramatic ex, however, acted like a full manicure set on my patience: nail file, scissors, clippers and all. At first I wondered how she could be so hysterical but little by little I caught up with her.

"Ah, Alice, don't be mad now! She'd cooked dinner for me, candles and all, and she opened the door in her erotic French-perfumed underwear. How could I leave?"

Sometimes he was really too much. At other times I could only envy my jealous mind's gift for creating a variety of detailed scenarios, imposing them onto reality, fully believing in them, and then starting furious fights.
Eventually our fights got physical.

"Please come back, Alice! I'm so sorry. I miss you, you know that?"

"There's no coming back, George. I let you off with the first slap. A second one always means that it won't be the last time. I've seen this with my parents already."

"But we love each other! It's so sad!"

Turning a page always feels sad. But not fucking turning it would be sadder.

Breaking up with George took too long. Healing afterward took even longer. All of me was a giant, gaping wound.

The first few days were bad. I was angry and determined for a fresh start without him, while my muscles still ached from the last time we'd had sex.

The next few months weren't bad; they were unbearable. Funny thing, I'd spent my whole life in this city, had my favorite haunts, but I'd taken George to them and now they seemed hollow without him. As I roamed the streets I'd stop with my eyes full of tears. I couldn't find the motivation to keep going. At every table I saw an empty chair meant for him. There was always a sad George-less chair. And every time, the light in my eyes grew weaker. I just couldn't bring myself to hate him. There might be only a single step between love and hate, but sometimes you're so spent by love that you don't have the strength to take even this tiny step.

"Why are you here? I told you, we're done."

"Stop it, Alice. I got you a little something."

The little something was a puppy. A substitute for our lost dream of having a kid together.

"I'm with somebody new, Alice. She's two months pregnant. But we can still have sex if you want…?"

I named the dog Art.

"I love the smell of you in the morning!" his shiny eyes promised.

To a dog even the stench of your dirty socks is a thousand times better than any French-perfumed underwear. Art couldn't tell me that he loved me, but he knew just how to show it to me. Perhaps if we humans didn't talk either, if we had tails to wag instead, we'd be much better at demonstrating our feelings. But I was only human. I didn't live up to Art's expectations, and ended up depriving him of my smell. I loved his loyal face, but it couldn't fill the emptiness in my heart, so I had to send him over to my sister. I'd decided to escape to another city. One that didn't look so much like George. The otherest city possible. In Signland. Honestly, I didn't believe I'd be able to forget him even there.

But then I met Jack.

"Jack was your third Great Love then?" Annie nonchalantly ticks off my heartbreaks on her fingers.

She doesn't read my stories herself anymore. She makes me read them out loud.

"Hell no, I've stopped counting. When you're immersed in it, love always seems greater than all the other feelings that preceded it. Each new relationship feels like the ultimate one… But that's all wrong. It's damn stupid to denounce the emotions we once used to burn with. We don't need to bury our memories forever, we just have to quit digging deeper and deeper…"

"Learning how to quit digging is an art unto itself," she says.

I'm relaxing in the bathtub; Annie gently caresses my skin with a sponge, adding a jug of hot water every now and then. I must've been here for hours, writing, reading, tiny drops of water from the faucet measuring the rhythm of my billowing thoughts. Everything is so white: the bathtub, the tiles, the reverberating sound in my head. Nothing in my love life has ever felt white. Crimson, dusty rose, mocha, indigo, raven black. Never white. This new clarity of mind – this new whiteness that comes with Annie – allows me to analyze the passion of the past without feeling broken. A dam has collapsed somewhere within me. I'm flooded with reflections on love.

For years my Heart behaved like someone who was never on my side. Living in my own body, but forever longing for the body of yet another man who'd screwed me over. That's how Heart is – a bit ungrateful, you know; you love it so much but it always loves someone else.

It cries self-breakingly deep in its cage made of ribs.

And you feel so much pity that eventually you're ready to go back out there, get hurt all over again, just to make Heart stop wailing in pain…

The knack is to realize that it's all bullshit. The heart is just an organ of the human body and its job is to pump blood, not to love. Hearts don't have feelings! Butterflies fluttering inside, worms eating away at our conscience, teddy bears in our memories … they're all Brain's doing. It's Brain who falls in love and makes Heart beat faster. And letting go is not about whether or not you stop loving. The secret to letting go is to distract Brain from this question altogether. Point it in the direction of other more meaningful things. They'll take away the pain, drop by drop. And even if any pieces of the unfortunate love remain, they'll now focus on the beautiful memories and the hope that each of you will separately find happiness.

"I figured so much out while I was living with depression. Now I'm at peace with all my past loves…"

"Oh yeah, your depression," Annie cuts into my monologue. "I want you to write about how I saved you."

"I need to tell the story of Venus Box first."

Broken

„But some people
are like crystal glasses,
and crystal glasses
are more fragile than porcelain."

I met Venus Box during my depression at home.

The spots on my thighs got me thinking: was all this solitude going to leave spots on my soul too? I decided to start socializing again, slowly; social media first.

Chris' Skype mood message:

It doesn't matter if you cry with pain or with joy – as long as your eyes glitter with tears, life is worth living!

Alice_in_Change: cool quote! Who said that?

Chris: Venus Box :)

Alice_in_Change: ?? I've never heard of it... Is it a book?

Chris: Venus Box doesnt write books. she has a blog

Chris: thebill.com

I clicked on the link, then couldn't stop reading. There was something about her style – naive yet thought-provoking. The full name of the blog was *Soul Heating Bill*. It started as a "leaflet in an envelope." Every month Venus would type the new issue on a typewriter; she then made copies, chose a neighborhood, and dropped the envelopes in people's mailboxes at random, "For those who miss receiving actual letters." But who was she to ignore the fact that everything in our *e*-veryday life has its virtual twin? She decided to upload *The Bill* online too.

Venus Box declared a peaceful protest against the media. She didn't dispute the need for it, but insisted that we mustn't rely solely on its content. It was often both manipulated and manipulative, and quite distant from our own reality. Venus wrote that what mattered most were the things we could perceive with our own senses, in the actual world around us, not via our screens.

"Let's get up from the couch, turn off our TVs and take a walk outside! We might see someone falling down with our own eyes, and there won't be a screen to stop us from reaching out a helping hand."

She lived up to her words. Her experiences with people felt authentic – I imagined her meeting them only minutes before she preserved their stories in *The Bill*.

"The media always tells us tales of one thousand and one deaths, but I believe that Good can be much more intriguing! Yes, it's crushingly sad that somewhere someone was shot, that children die. But what good is it to watch the news at seven every evening, filling our souls with the terror of so many tragedies from around the globe? Maybe Couch Potatoes need all this misery in order to feel virtuous. It reassures them of their own kindness and compassion – the pain from yet another heart-breaking report brings tears to their eyes, doesn't it? They must have a good heart then! But what's the point of it all? If we're not going to actually do something about these matters, if we don't plan to enroll as volunteers or start fundraising, it's no good shaking our heads over how

90

helpless we are. It reminds me of my grandmother's response every time I refused to eat when I was little: "There are starving children in Africa, and you're frowning at the meatballs like a snob!" As if cleaning my plate quickly enough would make it rain meatballs over Somalia.

"I will write about simple things that are no less gripping than tragedies," Venus promised. And she did. She knew how to make simple things sound exciting. She had many followers too: "ordinary people telling stories about other ordinary people, inspired by the revelation that no one is quite ordinary."

After I read all her blog posts with gusto, I got back to Chris.

> Alice_in_Change: You here?
> Chris: mhmm
> Alice_in_Change: This blog is really coo !!! Thanks
> for sharing ;) Didn't know you liked reading...
> Chris: well not rly but i like Venus Box
> Alice_in_Change: As a writer or...?
> Chris: my best-loved writer
> Chris: and my best-loved girl
> Alice_in_Change: Ahaa, I see :) Why haven't you
> told me about her?
> Alice_in_Change: Would your girl mind if you gave
> me her contact so I can let her know I'd like to
> subscribe to this mail version of The Bill...
> Chris: Alice...
> Chris: i'll give it to u but dont say it was me
> Chris: plz!
> Alice_in_Change: well... i won't write to her if it's a
> problem
> Chris: listn...
> Chris: you put it very nicely
> Chris: MY GIRL!
> Chris: only she doesnt want to be my girl

Chris: last time she asked me not to call any-
more...
Alice_in_Change: :(
Chris: im trying to do what she wants
Chris: although it hurts
Alice_in_Change: what happened? :(
Alice_in_Change: if you don't wanna talk about it,
it's ok...
Chris: i dont wanna talk about it
Alice_in_Change: ok
Chris: shes sick with smth but she doesnt want to
tell me what it is
Chris: she says she wont let me
Chris: waste my time with her
Chris: that i couldnt save her even if i wanted to...
Chris: i rly dont wanna talk about it...
Chris: i'll give u her contact but dont tell her
where u got it from!
Alice_in_Change: Ok... You cheer up, you hear me?
If it's you who's bound to save her, if you're going
to feel better after that... both of you... then it will
happen!!! If not, you can't force it...
Chris is typing...
Chris is typing...
Chris is typing...

I found Venus Box on Instagram. Her last post said:
My box reads ALREADY BROKEN

I cringed. I'm no stranger to grim statements but labeling yourself with something that shattered?

Regardless, I contacted her about my subscription. Venus replied and we started chatting. Her sense of humor was nice – black most of the time but always witty. Even when we talked about sad stuff, which happened a lot, there was a healthy amount of satire in what she said.

She also kept to herself at home, although she was still in high school. I couldn't fathom how she managed to excuse her absence from there, but she rarely went out. We spent entire nights awake, each of us at our own computer, doing our own stuff while chatting. Then we slept in till noon.

Once she reluctantly went to school and I was alone with my thoughts. "It doesn't matter if you cry with pain or with joy – as long as your eyes glitter with tears, life is worth living!" We'd bonded over this sentence but we were both cheating on it. Sure enough, withdrawing into yourself doesn't make your eyes glitter. You have your peace, true, but there's no one to make you really upset, or to make you laugh until you cry for that matter. I'd started to become one of those people I'd never understood – people with virtual friends. Unfelt, unmet. I wanted to see Venus's words written on her face too. So I left her a long paragraph, trying to get her to meet me.

Venus_Box: I just got back and read your message, Alice... I didn't realize it was so hard for you to have a "virtual friend," as you put it. I have lots of virtual friends and think it's normal. It even seems to me that online we can communicate more freely. Gone is the anxiety about how we look and it's easier to be honest. Sometimes we put masks on, but it is us who choose the mask, which means it doesn't contradict with our personality, it only shows another side, another version of ourselves... Anyways, I'm fine with meeting up, as it's so important to you. Only... I haven't told you anything about this, but I have a disease and Mia rarely lets me out to meet people. Please, don't ask for details about my

This Mia woman took her time giving permission. I saw Venus Box for the first time on February 14th. We didn't have anyone to celebrate Valentine's Day with, so it just made sense to hang out together.

Venus proposed that we meet in one of the cafés she'd come across while delivering the *Soul Heating Bill*. It was atmospheric, the sort of place that makes you unable to decide whether it's artsy or just kitsch. However, I felt comfortable the moment I went in. There wasn't room for too many people and I recognized Venus at once. But even if the place had been crowded, I still would've instantly known who she was. There was no body on her chair – only a huge pair of eyes, like in her pictures on social media. I smiled into those huge eyes, then sat down next to them.

"Hi!" her thin lips spoke thinly.

"Hi, Venus. Wow, your eyes are amazing! I've never seen anything like them!"

"Yeah, people always notice my eyes."

She looked so tiny and fragile. I guessed that had to do with her mysterious illness. I didn't say that, of course; guessed the way she looked had to do with her mysterious illness.

Right after the petty exchange of pleasantries we moved on to the real thing. It felt as if we were born to talk to each other. You know, one of those conversations where you think that what the other person says is exceptionally wise and interesting, and your own words seem exceptionally wise and interesting in return. I couldn't shut up for hours, but that's how I am normally – I talk a lot if I like the person. Venus couldn't shut up for hours either, even though my first impression of her was of a very shy girl.

We discussed her shyness too. She didn't feel confident enough to approach people and everyone at school misread that, thought she was stuck up. Sure they would. Society loves to talk about not discriminating against people based on their looks, but then again, society has always been a damn hypocrite. A beautiful girl never has the right to turn people down and walk away unpunished. If she turns down a guy, she's either too full of herself, or too stupid to appreciate his merits. If she isn't all over everyone all the time, she's not shy, oh no, she's definitely conceited. The Sour Grapes Syndrome.

Venus Box was a crystal glass.

Her box read ALREADY BROKEN.

"Sometimes I think it's easier for a girl to be happy if she's dumb or at least unattractive," I said.

"I know what you mean about the dumb part. People who aren't constantly asking questions about Meaning are not eternally tormented by the maddening lack of answers. Or by the maddening lack of Meaning… But what makes you think it's easier for unattractive girls to be happy? Beauty sets the rules in our reality, doesn't it, so isn't it harder for the unattractive to accomplish anything?" Venus and her big eyes asked.

"On the one hand, you're right. But it's no easier for women who are seen as attractive. They also have shit on their plates to deal with. It doesn't matter exactly how they're attractive – they might be beautiful in the classic sense, or rather charming, or they might have sex appeal. In any case, in order to achieve anything, they'll have to learn how to decline the lustful advances of all kinds of bullies and douchebags." I was speaking a hundred miles per hour already. That topic always ignited me. "And if a hot girl *does* eventually achieve something after all this trouble, there's a massive crowd of envious assholes to bitch about her supposedly having gone to bed with the right people. Society always gossips about women rather than men, and about hot women above all. Always. No wonder the proverb goes: 'Born under a lucky star!', and not 'Born sexy!' I don't think being sexy brings any luck."

As for the luck Venus and I were to have throughout our friendship… Fate gave us a hint of what was to come back then, when we first met.

At some point we were discussing the interior of the café. There was a lot to discuss: suitcases mounted on the walls, a clothesline with baby rompers strung up above the bar, glass-topped tables, under the glass – sand, shells and business cards left by customers. I didn't like the tacky upholstery of the booths (pink plush, blue plush, animal print plush), but I enjoy places where you can look around for hours and still find fascinating new details.

"Miss! Excuse me, miss!" A new fascinating detail startled us – a hoarse-voiced kid was approaching our table. "You're *so* beautiful, miss! C'mon, won't you buy one of my greeting cards?"

A young gypsy boy, maybe nineish. I asked for his name. "Ronaldo, after the soccer player," he said, chest puffed up with pride. The cards he sold were of the sort that had been very popular a decade ago, with tatty teddy bears on them. Venus said she used to collect them, so I decided to buy her a few. My excuse to give Ronaldo some money. He was such a cute kid!

"My phone's dead. What time is it?" Venus asked a bit later.

I glanced at the cuckoo clock on the wall. 10:10. It couldn't be that late. Apparently the clock was broken so I fished my phone out of my bag.

"20:20! Can you believe this?! I keep seeing repeating numbers every time I check the time!"

"Well... I'm hardly surprised," Venus shrugged with utter calmness. She even stopped tugging the sleeves of her sweater over her fingers – something she otherwise did all the time, as if attempting to hide every possible bit of herself. "Haha, don't worry, I got you! I see the numbers too and I've browsed for info. I'll send you more details later, but I'm pretty sure we're both at a critical juncture in our lives."

Funny thing, how awkward she was about everything mundane, and how sure of herself when it came to unearthly matters.

"There may also be a connection between the signs we're getting and our dreams," Venus kept on, "so you want to start writing down every dream you have."

"Sure. I always keep a journal on my nightstand any-way."

"I really have to go now! But I'll send you details!"

After leaving the café and walking a few blocks, we bumped into Ronaldo again. His face was stuck in an empty potato chip bag, huffing glue. The stack of greeting cards was left on top of a power box so he could focus on the job.

DANGER
HIGH VOLTAGE

The bag seemed enormous in Ronaldo's small hands. It wanted to devour him whole. Only his eyes looked bigger than the bag; larger than the world. My destiny was to come across huge eyes that evening, and my own eyes were already welling up with saltiness. I felt an urge to grab the little guy. Shake him roughly and then give him a hug. Make him stop! But I just kept walking.

"There's no point in telling him off, right? He won't hear a thing," even I could barely hear my voice, it trembled so badly.

"At least he had some chips before he used the bag for the glue." Venus's lips warped into what was supposed to be a smile, but her eyes were even fuller than mine. Boats of suffering children sailed in there.

Excerpts from Alice's Dream Journal #1

February 20th

In my dream I was running late for an exam. I was my present age, so I should have finished high school several years ago, but suddenly a terrible realization hit me. I hadn't finished anything. I didn't have a diploma because for the past two years I hadn't set foot in a single math class. Cold sweat on my forehead. Was it possible that I'd never completed my secondary education??? The next moment I found myself at school, trying to persuade my math teacher to give me a passing grade. The school building looked weird. The upper floors were the same as usual, but the ground floor resembled a hospital ward. The teacher was a bearded man with a mustache, although in my sleep I was convinced that it was good old Mrs. Raeva. She told me to come back the following day to sit the exam.

Right after that – obviously it was the following day – I couldn't leave home because I didn't have anything to wear. Home wasn't the place where we live now, it was the apartment where we used to live when I was young. I started crying. I was running late for the exam, but I didn't have any clothes and I was embarrassed to go out naked. The bearded and mustached Mrs. Raeva showed up on my doorstep. I looked at her through the spyhole. "Put this on," she said, holding up a pink bra with three straps. I firmly refused to wear a pink bra. I didn't mind the number of straps though – in my dream it seemed normal. Mrs. Raeva started trying to convince me that it wasn't a problem if I went out with no clothes on. I just needed to put my shoes on and then people wouldn't realize I was naked, she said. But I couldn't do that either. I remembered that I'd poured coffee into my shoes that morning and they were no good.

Then I started painting. I painted for a long time and eventually I got two landscapes that I put on my feet. I headed to school like that – with paintings on instead of shoes. Next, I was on the bus but somehow watching it from behind at the same time. I could see the number on the back window. It was line number five.

Normally I don't bother trying to interpret the meaning of my dreams, but then again, normally I forget them seconds after I wake up. This one I've remembered in detail for two days in a row now, so I decided to take a peek in a dream interpretation book.

Exam – if you're anxious before an exam, you'll experience the fear of failure.

Being late – interesting experience; or someone in your close circle envies you.

School – someone's secret will be revealed; it might be your own secret, and it might disgrace you; another interpretation treats dreaming of a school as a sign of childhood insecurities that haven't been overcome yet.

100

House where you lived as a child – a desire to start your own family; a need for help and protection.

Dreaming that you are naked – you will be in good health but be cautious – someone might disgrace you. What, again?

In summary: clearly it's time for me to find myself a man, overcome my insecurities and be disgraced. In my personal opinion, this dream simply means that I'll never rid myself of the disgust I felt for math at school.

March 4th

I dreamed that a gray mouse just stood there and watched me.

March 5th

For a second night I dreamed that a gray mouse was just standing there, staring and staring.

The dream book is a bit vague about the exact meaning of mice. It could be an enemy.

April 17th

For a while I flew over a calm sea (or lake) with an abundance of beautiful little islands scattered across its emerald surface. My stomach turned, and it was a wonderful feeling. Then I landed in a strange man's arms. He carried me along several deserted streets before laying me down in an empty bathtub. We had sex. That feeling wasn't bad either.

I don't think I need the dream book for this one. It's pretty obvious that I need more flying and sex.

More Pieces
of the
Looking-Glass World

I didn't see Venus for a while after we first met. She sent me two *Soul Heating Bills* though. The first was about Ronaldo; the second, about me. Venus wrote that she'd met someone else with depression like hers. She'd also met someone who laughed more than anyone else.

The depressed person and the laughing person – they were both me.

There was detailed information about repeating numbers too. The most popular belief was that they were guiding signs from angels. They could mean different things: that we were moving in the right direction, or in the wrong one; that we needed to revive the connection with our soul; or pay attention to something we missed. Venus wrote about a numerological methodology used by Pythagoras too, and also about how all this related to the indigo children – the next stage in human evolution, people with a dark blue aura who emerged in the late 60s, extremely sensitive and aware. She thought I was one of those special indigo kids. But frankly, I've never been much into discussions about spirit and light.

Besides, I don't like angels. They're so boring. Even hookers are more fascinating than angels.

Still, I was touched by Venus's admiration for me.

Before I saw her again, I discovered the truth about her condition.

A few years ago we moved into an apartment building with many stories. Many stories indeed! I frequently heard someone throwing up in the apartment upstairs. It happened almost every night, the noise rumbling and scratching through the piping. For a while I couldn't tell if it was a woman or a man – apparently the sound of puking is universal. I supposed it was a man who got drunk and vomited on a regular basis.

One night it sounded more like a woman. I was in the bathroom where it could be heard distinctly. I stopped the shower. The spasms were just finishing and the person started crying. It *was* a woman. Unable to bear listening any longer, I fled the bathroom and called my sister, needing to share the haunting experience.

"She has bulimia," Sis spilled the diagnosis out casually, as if it was trivial, a sparrow at the window or something.

I knew about bulimia, of course, but I hadn't imagined it to be as common as sparrows at windows.

"What, you don't have any bulimic friends?" Sis asked.

"Nope, I don't think so. Enlighten me, please!"

My sister was in fifth grade when she found out that one of her besties threw up every day. Gabriela. They were in the same modern ballet class.

I remembered that ballet class well. I had been at the height of puberty when my sister attended and my folks had a hard time persuading me to join them anywhere, so I saw my sis perform just once. She was better than the rest of the kids, and I'm not just saying that because I love her. She had it in her ever since she was a toddler. You know how most kids dance, right? Uncoordinated and clumsy. That was how the other students in the ballet class moved, whereas my sister had the grace of a ballerina. They'd put her in the back row though. She didn't have the body of a ballerina. Not too chubby, but she couldn't pass for *slim* either. Disgusted by this attitude, I left the gym in a thunder.

Sis gave up on dancing soon afterward. The teacher constantly pressured her to get skinnier, and young Gabriela revealed the secret to losing weight. My sis tried puking too, choking over the toilet bowl at home. No one noticed, but she freaked out and decided she was done with ballet. Eventually she lost weight naturally, but ever since then she's only danced when she's alone in her room.

Gabriela eventually became a model. And she had bulimia, apparently. Sis knew several girls like her and painted a detailed picture of their illness for me. The picture was sad.

Drugs. Smoking. Booze. Gambling. Gaming. Self-injuring. Sex. Or porn. Social media. Coca-Cola, for Christ's sake! As if all the other addictions we've developed aren't enough, eating disorders have become rampant too.

Anorexia, bulimia and hyperphagia, which is basically binge eating minus the purging. Weird and misunderstood, they're the new bonfire of vanity, or at least that's how most people see them. Judgmental tutting, the notion that there's nothing more to these issues than body obsession. The sufferers' inner drive is quite different though. In their big eyes, abstinence from food equals denial of the body, which equals a rebellion against everyone else's vanity. Against a whole world that tortures them with ads of slimming products, followed by so many food ads, yummy-looking, greasy, enticing. A world that only knows how to consume.

The families of the disordered also burn on the pyre. Victims of bulimia and anorexia decline direct help and at the same time throw indirect accusations at everyone around them for not helping. They don't do it on purpose. It's just how things work.

"And they're all so intelligent!" my sister said in conclusion.

No doubt they were. I'd long figured out that the most intelligent people were especially prone to addictions. Forever dying with questions, they'd cling to anything that feigned Meaning.

"It's so hard for them to fight their illness because they kinda have this love for it," Sis went on. "It makes them feel different, almost enlightened. I've read online forums about eating disorders. The girls there go as far as using pet names for their condition: anorexia is called Ana, bulimia is Mia. Imagine that!"

The name sliced through my brain. Could it be the same Mia who'd been bullying Venus all along?

"Oh shit! I might have a bulimic friend after all! There's this girl I met recently… I know she's ill but she won't tell me what she has."

"Let me take a look at her Instagram!"

"Wh-what?!"

"Tell me her name and I'll find her. I'll tell you right away if she's bulimic. Their accounts stand out from miles away."

It only took a couple of pictures for my sister to confirm bulimia. She sent me links to some of her friends' profiles, and she was damn right – they all had a lot in common. Pictures of their big eyes. Of other people's big eyes. Pictures of various parts of their bodies, all of them shockingly thin. The skinniest possible full-length pictures, or pictures taken from above so that their heads seemed much bigger than their bodies. Pictures and illustrations of little girls. Sad, bewildered, crumpled like embryos. Gloomy postures with gloomy captions. And the occasional badge with some positive message.

"Fuck! I have to help her!"

"Sis, I don't like to say this, but I doubt there's anything you can do. I've been trying to help Gabbie for years. Feels like I'm fighting with Gabriela herself, not with the illness! She says she wants to get better, we make plans, all sorts of plans… And in the end she's back hugging the toilet, throwing up all our efforts."

"But you still don't give up, right? You're not just standing by indifferently, holding her hair back while she's puking. I have to try too. They need help, not sympathy!"

Venus_Box hadn't been online for several days. I tried to call. Phone off. But I was determined to give my support, even if she didn't want it. I checked the return address on the *Soul Heating Bill* and set off looking for Venus first thing in the morning.

My own depression melted away in the glorious weather outside.

Spring is the best pharmaceutical scientist. The only one who knows how to transform trees into antidepressants.

I skipped down the streets, the smile on my face skipping up and down with me. People stared, but I didn't bother to hide that I was laughing by myself. They laughed in response.

Strangers always notice your smile.

Just as I arrived at the address, a mother struggled to push a stroller through the front door. I held it open for her, then took the opportunity to sneak in. It was an old aristocratic building. High ceilings going nowhere, wooden window frames painted in white latex, the expectation of awe-inspiring tiled stoves in intricately decorated living rooms, the evocative smell of dusty wet stairs. Nothing like the mundane graffiti scratched on the shit-brown walls of my apartment building: football team names, uneducated political slogans, and thesauruses for genitalia slang too. Something in the air made me realize that Venus was part of a world unknown to me. I had no idea how she'd react to my unexpected visit.

Much to my dismay, she threw her arms around my neck, all excited and chirpy, quite different from the girl I'd met on February 14th. This new Venus had color and curves too. Her cheekbones no longer looked as if they hurt all the time, as if you could cut your finger on them. She'd obviously indulged in food in the time we hadn't seen each other, and when she didn't deprive herself of guilty pleasures, her mood clearly improved. She happily pulled me in by the hand.

There was more to her blossoming too. Venus flooded me with psyched reports of the past few evenings. I was already familiar with the beginning of the story. It starred Chris. Venus told me there was a guy who was in love with her, but she'd asked him to leave her alone.

"Um… Chris is a friend of mine actually. He's the one who told me about your blog." Although I'd specifically promised not to tell Venus this, it felt weird to keep it a secret now that she'd mentioned Chris anyway.

"Oh, really?" She just shrugged and carried on with her story.

Chris came up with the idea to serenade Venus. As he couldn't sing, he contacted a Troubadour Agency and they sent a guy named Tino to croon under her balcony.

"He sings like an angel! And he looks like one too!"

Once the serenade was over, Venus had a chat with Tino from her balcony. She found out his job was to play the guitar and sing every night until "the chick gets back with her ex." By the look of how impressed this particular chick was with the troubadour, I doubted Chris stood a chance.

                              Soul Heating Bill
                              May

Tino

Did you pay your Soul Heating Bill this month? Did you do a deed of kindness without letting anyone know it was you? Did you talk to a stranger because they looked like they really needed someone to talk to? Did you put at least one uplifting story on a piece of paper? Did you slip it into a random mailbox?

If you did even one of these things, then you have paid your Soul Heating Bill. And here is my story for the month.

I first met Tino a couple of days ago. I wish I could meet him for the first time every day. He turns the world around. If you passed him by on an escalator and he stood still, there's a chance you might miss him. The slightest movement on his part, however, will blow your mind. You'll be sucked into his energy field and you won't be able, or willing, to tear yourself away.

Tino is a graffiti artist. He told me the most inspiring story of how he became one.

His dad lived in one of the high-rise districts. On one fateful day in the late 1980s, he saw Elsa sitting on a bench alongside the neighboring apartment building. The new kid on the block shone like a sun among the other girls, and Tino's dad was swept off his feet. His first love. At first sight. After a while he gathered the courage to go forth and invite the lady of his heart to the movies. Her friends, perched on the benches like a flock of mockingbirds, cawed a condition, "Only if you give 'er a ride there!"

"I will," Tino's dad said. He arrived for their date on his worn-out skateboard, put Elsa on it and thus took her to the movie theater, telling her jokes the whole way. That was how he stole her heart.

A few years later, Elsa and Tino's dad had a fight. She accused him of misleading her with his skateboard ploy; he got her to believe that he was a romantic soul, but since they started dating he hadn't bought her a single flower. The next morning she went out and found a crowd of neighbors discussing a huge drawing of a rose that had appeared overnight on the side of their apartment building. The drawing is long gone, but to this day locals will point you in the right direction if you ask for the building with the rose.

Tino came into the world a decade afterward. He had always felt proud that his very own father had drawn the first piece of graffiti in our post-socialist city for his very own mother. As a matter of fact, his dad performed no more such feats, but Tino decided he wanted to be a proper writer himself. He came up with a nickname and started tagging while he was still in primary school, but he wasn't much of an artist and he didn't feel he was entitled to do big pieces outside. So he practiced at home.

Tino told me that making graffiti is like being in love. It comes with the same ache to be perfect, the same self-doubt, the constant mood swings. At one moment you are happy because love makes you think you are the greatest; next thing you know, your confidence has vacated you and the very same love infects you with an all-predominating feeling of inferiority, as if you'll never be good enough.

Tino told me about the two most important walls in his room: one for hate, one for love. When he's angry he thrashes the wall of hate with his fists instead of taking it out on whoever angered him. On the wall of love, he practices his graffiti art. He practiced for a long time before eventually deciding that it was not his gift. "That's why on the wall of love there's pain and woe too. And on the wall of hate there's some graffiti. Drawn in blood. Sometimes I hit it till my fists bleed!"

I think I am in love. I want to kiss all his blood away. I want to be the inspiration that will make Tino love his murals.

In fact, he has found a way around his lack of skill in drawing. He specializes in stencil graffiti. It doesn't require any exceptional gifts; you create something you like in Photoshop, print it out, cut out a stencil and then all you need to do is spray over it with your can. What matters is the idea behind your image and your ability to spray it on the street without getting caught. Once Tino discovered this method, he felt he was ready to leave the room. He started stenciling on buildings in his neighborhood. Then the neighborhood felt too small. Next, the city felt too small. In the beginning, he saved his pocket money to buy spray paint cans. After he graduated, he got a job and used the money to travel around Europe. Every month he painted in a new city. He told me that when he was in London, he even got to meet the great Banksy. Mysterious Banksy who is famous across the world yet remains anonymous. Well, Tino knows who he is. He and Banksy had a long talk about graffiti culture there, on the streets of London. It all sounds incredible, but why would he lie to me?

Tino's whole life is a paradise of excitement! Sometimes I have crazy thoughts, like fervently wishing to turn into a keychain – Tino's keychain – so that I could be with him all the time. This is awfully scary. So is the thought that if something more happens between us, the magic of our first evenings together and the serenades under my balcony will forsake us forever...

"Do you seriously speak with this Tino from your balcony every time? Why don't you go downstairs or invite him to come up?"

Venus shivered, a ripple of disgust crossing her face. "Look how fat I am! I can't show myself to him like this!"

"Venus, I… Actually I want to talk to you about that. I know you're bulimic."

Suddenly she was crying. She wasn't a woman in love anymore, she was a kid and I didn't know what to do but take the kid in my arms. Trembling little bird that she was, so fragile despite the new curves. Her crying went on forever, and in the end she was still weeping but managed to talk through her sobs. She told me about her mother – a Russian actress, singer and ballerina who named Venus after the goddess of love but failed badly in actually loving her.

"When I was little it was all so easy. 'Beautiful and talented, just like her mother!' that's what people would always say."

Then Venus got older and let everyone down by quitting ballet. Fuck ballet, is it always a catalyst for girls who start puking? Being exposed to an audience just wasn't Venus's thing. People stopped shrilling that she looked like her mother and started whispering about the differences instead. "At her age… And look at her…"

"There was only one person who found me more interesting than my mother... Disgusting!"

This statement crept into her story like a hateful ghost, then she moved on without explaining. She told me how her mother traveled all the time and would leave Venus all alone in their huge apartment for days or even weeks on end. It seemed that the only time she did pay attention to her daughter was when she criticized her for every pound she'd put on. She was never bothered when Venus lost weight dramatically.

She'd silently approve of her appearance, then point out that their pet poodle needed to go on a diet.

"I don't get this whole thing with losing weight and then putting it back on," I admitted. "Isn't it only one of the two, anorexia *or* bulimia?"

Venus explained that she had different periods. At times she'd be anorexic. Merciless starvation, with no chewing gums or even toothpaste, because: "Venus, chewving gum is vith calories!" She rolled her eyes as she imitated her mother's accent.

Venus's grandmother frequently stocked the fridge with supplies. In an anorexic bout, Venus would give everything to the poodle. And although she barely put anything in her own mouth, she'd climb up and down the stairs several times a day to get fitter. She sometimes fainted, but kept on.

Then there came the times of bulimia. She'd eat elephantine amounts of food, then kneel in front of the toilet bowl. Whenever she ran out of proper food, she'd turn to eccentric concoctions. Mashed potatoes with Oreos. Yogurt with ketchup. She even fancied the dog's food sometimes.

"I'm obsessed with it. In my binging episodes, all I think about is what I can eat; in my starving episodes, it's all about what I can't eat. The worst is when you've spent days in a row on nothing but fresh orange juice, and then you have a dream in which you're eating chocolates, one after the other, one after the other, until the whole box is gone… Oh, the feeling of guilt before you realize it was only a dream and you didn't ruin your life!"

Venus had kept Mia a secret for so long. Now she obviously needed to throw up all the disturbing details of living with her.

"In my worst anorexic fit all my bones stuck out, and little hairs, like the ones newborns have, started growing out of my skin. Maybe that's what I aim for subconsciously – to be as tiny as a newborn because when I was tiny I was happy. Everything is so nice and easy when you're a child!"

True. Life is much easier for kids: you can talk to yourself, have imaginary friends, fall in love with cartoon characters. Grown-ups find all of it sweet.

Once you grow up, however, they start thinking it's sick.

"When we were kids, we loved the story of Karlsson-on-the-Roof," I said. "A few years later, a friend of ours became

Karlsson-who-jumped-off-the-roof. Since then, every time we try to fall, we end up falling. But you know what? I believe we can totally conquer anything!"

I stayed over at Venus' and all night we tried to figure out how to beat Mia. We decided to spend all of our time together. This way Venus wouldn't have to be alone in her high-ceilinged cage with her thoughts about food. We decided on something else too, and it wasn't so innocent.

"My grandma sent me to rehab once and I spoke with many girls in my situation. Some of them said they use Annie and she's of some help. Annie? You know who I mean?"

"I've met her once…"

The next day we were already searching for Annie. I spoke to the guy who'd introduced us a few years earlier. He said he hadn't hung out with her for a while, and suggested that I do the same. Eventually Venus called Chris. He didn't like the idea at all, but his desire to please Venus was stronger than any concern. He dug out one of Annie's phone numbers for us. We dialed and the voice at the other end said he'd fetch her.

An hour later we were at the place the dealer had chosen – the back entrance of a school. Near us a power box was bathing in the sun.

DANGER!
HIGH VOLTAGE
DO NOT TOUCH!

I remembered Ronaldo.

"Why are you so attached to Venus? Because she's even more fucked up than you are?"

Early morning. Annie and I are sitting at a chess table in the park. We were at a club, but then Venus invited some people we'd just met over to her place. Annie said I'd rather come here to write. I can hear the whistle of the 4 a.m. bird. My knowledge of ornithology is quite poor, I don't really know which species of bird it is, but I know it's the 4 a.m. one. Depression, insomnia, Annie. I've been up through so many nights that I can tell apart the bird sounds of each early hour.

I'm probably the only person in the whole park, but no place feels vacant with Annie. Her daring eyes scrutinize me from across the chess table.

"Venus is pretty fucked up, yeah," I say calmly. "She belongs to my tribe – Those Who Search for Meaning."

"And what other tribes are there?"

Annie's old trick. Gets me to describe everything in detail, even though she knows perfectly well what I mean from the very beginning. When I start elaborating aloud, I can hear with my own ears that something in my reasoning is not right. That's exactly her goal.

"Those Who Don't Search for Meaning and Those Who Have Found Meaning... You're damn right, Annie, ours is the tribe that makes happiness most unlikely. Almost unthinkable."

My life's been pretty wild these past few weeks. Or maybe it's been months already? I get lost in my winding thoughts, as always with Annie, only this time I trip into thinking about the wrong path.

The wrong path. You look for Meaning and you're misunderstood. Different. An outcast. So much more special than everyone who's not lost. You get hooked on something; a bad habit. At first, it makes you feel even more misunderstood, more of an outcast. Even more special. You like that, blind to the fact that you're slowly becoming a clone. Just like everyone else who's hooked on this particular something. In the beginning, it seems to be the only part of life you can control – what food to stuff yourself with, when to get high, whether to bring a bottle of whiskey home… With time, the genie in the bottle gets to control everything, and you're no one anymore. The Meaning is gone, completely. You've fooled yourself that with friends like Annie, Mia, Boro, or Jack you could be yourself in someone else's world. But you can't. You have to learn how to be yourself on your own. Only then can you join the tribe of Those Who Have Found Meaning.

"You ready?"

Annie has sensed the direction of my thoughts. She doesn't like it. She's all about glitter, firecrackers and lace; doesn't want to know about broken people and shit. She likes to be seen as the savior. Likes me to talk about how she makes me feel superhuman.

"Yes. I'm ready to tell your story now."

Panting and feverish, I start writing about how we landed head-first in the world of drugs. The 4 a.m. whistle is gone.

It's probably seven already. People are jogging around and I avoid their eyes. Annie is all over me. I wonder if they can see her. What they think about us. "What do you care," she chuckles. Right. I don't care. I keep writing on the chess table. Can't seem to use the past tense anymore. Past tense is too cold. Too final. And writing about Annie is too personal.

She's all about now.

A No-Tea Party

So many looking-glass worlds.

Mirror worlds.

Different worlds.

A whole new world in the distorting mirror of eating disorders. Every bone seems obese.

If you direct the mirror at your inner self, the world there is also entirely different from everything that surrounds you.

One particular mirror world is bigger than the rest. The world of nightclubs; an octopus, its tentacles spread over the entire planet. The restroom is a sanctuary there. It's furnished with huge mirrors so ladies can powder their noses. It's furnished with something else too: all types of horizontal mirrored surfaces, sometimes polished black, from which anyone can snort powder. White powder. Or yellowish. Light pink. Never noticed the mirrored surfaces in nightclub restrooms? Well, if you go looking for them, they'll be there. I promise.

And when you go out with Annie, you damn sure look for them.

The first few times she always comes with a discount, she's intense and stays for quite a while. Venus and I, we're psyched to play the game, all in. I've read that different personality types enjoy different types of drugs. We're clearly the amphetamine type.

She seems harmless. Nothing like what I imagined using would be like. Annie doesn't feel heavy, dark, trippy, or even addictive. She doesn't make me hallucinate or die. I don't want to die. I don't want to live in a make-believe world. She helps keep my spirits up, that's all. I can't say I'm happy with her, but I don't have the feeling of unhappiness either. Come to think of it, I haven't been feeling much of anything lately. Which is good. Besides, unlike with booze or weed, Annie doesn't make it seem like my behavior or my body will fail me.

I really like her, and Venus does too. Every Friday night, we hop on the Annie-go-round, and it's always a riot, celebrated with a no-tea party.

It starts in front of the mirror at home.

Put makeup on your eyes. Conceal your eyes. I don't want anyone to see the scars in my gaze. The cold steel of people's souls has turned my stare into cold steel too. I still smile like before, but my naked eyes flash arrows of anger. With makeup on, all they do is look beautiful. I don't want to be deep anymore. I just want to look good. When you've lost everything else, all you have left is your beauty. So I pose in front of the mirror until I'm completely satisfied with my looks.

Then I go out.

On my way downstairs I check:
purse,
keys,
phone…
and a smile!

Venus is waiting for me. Downtown. We're taking over the Mirror World.

The real world is overwhelmed by the Big Bad Crisis, but we're better than that. We float above people's petty concerns. One perk of not having an income is that you don't have to worry about your income decreasing. We scrape together enough cash for clubbing. It doesn't matter which of us finds the money, it's "ours" by default. Annie takes her share of the loot to join in. We lock ourselves in the restroom – all three of us, one cubicle – then we dash out, exhilarated and hooting, dancing our way to the dance floor. I don't care if I drink, or how much. I'm never too wasted with Annie. She's a better dance teacher than alcohol, too. Moves me in ways that I wasn't capable of before. Perfectly rhythmic, or at least that's how it feels to me. I like every kind of music when I'm with Annie. I've even come to appreciate electronic raves – obviously I just needed someone like her to clarify things. She waves her pointer, showing my brain where to put the individual elements of house music to make it enjoyable. Utterly so.

We're always the last to leave. The urge to dance evaporates as soon as we open the door of the club. *Who switched the sun on?* We squint in disgust. We are vampires, missing the night, but we wait snakelike in the light for the next evening. We don't feel like going home.

We're never alone. The smiles we scatter around in the clubs and out on the streets attract all kinds of weirdos. God knows why we find it fascinating to have conversations with them. We talk nonsense, of course.

Then it's Saturday night and the no-tea party is back on. Again, we slip into a club, into the cozy breath of the crowd, into the warmth of people's bodies. Our batteries are running low now, but Annie's always here, caring, ready to offer her restroom recharge. Another night of energy and dancing, our bodies spinning around…

Disco balls.
Spinning around with their mirror scales.
Spinning…
Disco balls.
Our bodies.

It's Sunday morning already and we can barely move, but Annie won't let us fall asleep; not yet. We lie down for hours – we can't even tell if they pass quickly or slowly. Eventually we die, and we're not to be resurrected until the following evening. We don't recover from our sleepless marathons until Wednesday. We don't feel like doing anything, and we don't have anything to do, for that matter. On Thursday we're fine, and on Friday we start preparing for another no-tea party.

Friday, Saturday, Sunday. Three days of no eating, drinking without getting drunk, unholy partying.

"You're Annie-go-round, a jolly carousel, and I can get off whenever I want!"

Venus loses weight rapidly without any effort. So do I. She told me once that she used to take loads of laxatives before, besides throwing up, in an attempt to get rid of the food she'd devoured. "It's like you're peeing from the wrong hole. Day after day." Well, she doesn't have to pee from the wrong hole now. Annie makes us lose our appetite and gives us false energy to exhaust our bodies to the limit.

It took Chris a full month to give up on the serenades. Long before he stopped paying the agency, Venus had already got her troubadour's number. I feel bad for Chris, yet I can't help but find some humor in this ridiculous situation. The Wallet, foolish with love, pays Tino, and then Tino hits on the Wallet's love interest with his sexy guitar and sensual voice. A relationship with such a street Romeo can hardly do Venus any good, but her relationship with Mia is worse. She needs someone to distract her, make her feel good. We both agree she needs a man…

"… And you chose some macho musician!"

"It's him I want. What can I do?"

As simple as that.

Venus lacks the ability to ever feel slim enough, but she calls Tino as soon as she finds herself "bearably not-fat". It's Friday night again and he says he's jamming in a karaoke bar called The Mockingbird. I imagine he goes there to practice his troubadour skills.

"Get your cute asses up here!" he says over the phone. His voice is nice, raspy and cool; a good casting choice for a candy-bar commercial. I can't imagine him with Venus though, her manner of speech more on the literary side.

We have just enough money for Annie and a single whiskey each. This means we don't have any for a taxi, so getting our asses up there consists of one long walk. When we finally get to the bar, Tino has usurped the stage with a ballad. The guy really oozes charisma. Venus gapes at him in a way that has me expecting big red hearts to appear in her eyes. She wiggles hello. Her other palm sweats in mine. I laugh, putting a hand to her chest.

"Wow! Good thing the bass is up! Otherwise everyone would hear your heart thumping!" I whisper in her ear.

Tino sees that and smiles from the spotlight – the typical lopsided smirk of a womanizer. He leaves the stage mid-song. Comes up to us. Kisses both of our hands while still holding the mic. His hand-kiss feels light but kind of suggestive too. As if you've just signed a contract with him. A lengthy stare in my eyes. A lengthy stare in Venus's eyes. All the while he somehow manages to keep singing and reading the lyrics on the screen behind us. Then he leans on the bar next to Venus, and the rest of the song is all hers. Poor jittery Venus! She can't help fiddling with her hair, and what's worse, her desperate attempts to refrain from doing so are all too obvious. Her blush glows in the dark.

When Tino's next song comes up, Venus is outside, speaking to her mom on the phone. He takes the opportunity to sing to me too. Eyes on mine the whole time, those wet eyes that make you feel like the hottest woman on earth … until you realize he can switch the wetness on and off like car blinkers. By the end of the evening, he'll sing a few more songs, each time focusing on a different lady, making her feel like the hottest woman on earth.

At some point I go to the restroom. I do my thing and when I come out of the cubicle, sniffing intently, Tino is at the sink. Looks at me in the mirror. Taps his nose and gives me a wink.

"You on speed? Come on hon, lay it on me. I seriously doubt you've got the dough for snow."

"How the hell can you tell? Is it that obvious?"

"It's your pupils, sweetheart," he takes hold of my chin, his touch gentler than I expect, turns my face toward the mirror. "They're bigger than five cent coins, you know! Plus, Venus and you? You can't keep your fingers off your noses. That bill you took out to pay back there? It instantly rolled into a tube … its usual shape, I'd guess. See, I used to snort a lot, you know, so I see things. I'm off now though. Figured I had enough energy for fun without dealing with the dope. Not to mention the goons who almost chopped my ears off for pushing on their turf… Anyways, it took months to stop rubbing my goddamn nose! But better ditch the bill, sweetheart – you can get all kinds of diseases like that! You know what you should really use is straws… That's the key here. You gotta be a rookie if you don't know this already. Am I right?"

"Yup. A rookie – that's me. But I don't plan on sticking with it for too long. It's just what's going on now."

"It's pointless, hon! I mean, what do you want with the dope anyway?"

"Well, I have things going on. Shitty things. It keeps me from thinking about them. Cheers me up."

"Just you wait. Once you get used to it, the cheer's gone, baby. Just watch out for the other stuff... Good old powder's not that bad. I'm just saying, you know, if you offered me a little right now, I could maybe do with a line."

I like it when people are straightforward about what they want. I say I'll cut him a line. We have to go to the men's restroom for that but I don't care – when you're with Annie, restrooms become sexless. Who'd think about sex as she lies down on the mirrored surface, naked, spread thin! Everyone longs to touch her and nothing else...

Tino touches her clumsily, however, and the last specks of Annie melt into the wet spots on the tiles.

"Shit! My bad. Pouring one for the dead, I guess... You gonna lick the bag?"

'What?! I'm not licking any bags! I'm not a junkie, you know!"

"Seriously, and I don't mean no disrespect hon, but I say you're a junkie alright. Yeah, hon. A junkie. What were you thinking? That only guys on H are junkies? You got it wrong, baby. You become a junkie the first time you call the dealer. You following me here? Once *you* start looking for Annie, instead of *her* looking for you, you're done for! I'm just saying, you know? That's why I deleted all the scumbag dealers from my contacts and now I only get by if somebody treats me – just a little, every now and then, taking it easy..."

I don't like being called a "junkie." I object. Tino offers his version of comfort.

"Relax, would you? You're a junkie, so what? No biggie. Everybody and their mother gets high these days."

Some comfort. But I know it's all true.

At some point in life there comes a moment when you realize what a huge number of people do drugs. Kids do drugs; more than ever before, it seems. Venus told me she often sees students snorting in the bathrooms at her fancy school. Many of her classmates call the dealer before they go out clubbing with their fake IDs. Now, I'm not saying every kid out there keeps a syringe in their back pocket, but many have sniffed powder or at least eaten candy.

Or what about all the stoned souls in showbiz and art? Strawberry Fields Forever. Stephen King. Writers do drugs. Cartoonists do drugs. Could a sober person come up with the concept of ninja turtles named after Renaissance artists who live in the sewers, feed on pizza, have a rat for a master, and a pink brain for an enemy? And that show is old school, they make them even crazier these days.

Of course, artistic minds are kooky even without drugs. I doubt Lewis Carroll was a junkie, yet he created a skillful description of every junkie's paradise. I know many people who earnestly envy his Alice. The girl gobbles down mushrooms and suspicious-looking cakes, and drinks one psychoactive potion after another. She swells, then she shrinks. A caterpillar smoking hookah on a mushroom. What else could a user wish for?

Yes, true artists are kooky as they are. Maybe everyone else is simply trying to find the same unhinged inspiration in drugs… I was shocked to find out that quite a few of my acquaintances were close to Annie or to some of her sisters without me ever noticing. Surpriiise! Have people started doing drugs all of a sudden, I wonder, or have I been blind all along? I can spot the signs now because they're all over me too.

I've stayed away from this drug-packed world for a surprisingly long time. Nay, I've stayed *right in* this drug-packed world but have been oblivious to its powders, to the traces they leave on restroom trash cans, all of them with smooth, polished-mirror lids.

God knows how many more layers of the world have eluded me. God knows what else happens in my very own city, right under my very own nose.

I want to be God. I want to know.

I refuse to be ignorant, so I'll see as much as possible. No matter what it takes. And I won't look from the outside – I'll see it all from the inside, up close. Annie is my pick from the realm of drugs. I have this urge to find out: what does it feel like to sneeze when you're with her? To have sex when you're with her? I have to explore. And I keep exploring. My life is measured in Fridays, Saturdays, Sundays. Endless no-tea escapades sprinkled with her feverish, bitter-to-the-throat, sweet-to-the-mind flavor.

Drained.
Bleeding with exhaustion.
Almost ill.

I'm a wreck every time I get back from a no-tea party. Still, I'm willing to pay the price over and over again in order to get my fix of Friday-Sunday euphoria.

On my way upstairs I check:
purse,
keys,
phone,
cringey smile.
Everything's here. My soul must be here somewhere too.

132

I'm not worried about losing anything. My time, perhaps, as usual, but I'll fret over time tomorrow. Or another, worthier day; although I can't see the outlines of any worthier days on the horizon. I don't feel like getting a job. All I want is for everyone to leave me alone so I can go on with my explorations.

Back home.

Turn the light on, turn my eyes off. I can do this at last. No one to scrutinize my gaze here, and claim to have found what they thought they'd find. In here, my eyes are free to die out without anyone rushing to rescue them just to feel like a hero. *Why don't all heroes go and save themselves first?*

Two last things. *Brush your teeth, go to bed!*

As I brush I study my eyes in the mirror. Annie's made them look unnaturally large – the eyes of an anime princess… Only this princess doesn't mean to save anyone, let alone the whole world. And she doesn't think she needs saving. Am I repeating myself?

Drained.
Bleeding with exhaustion.
Almost ill.

Once again on my way back from a no-tea party, once again a mess.

Purse,
phone,
keys?!

This time the keys aren't here. I must have left them on the shoe rack inside the apartment. Inside, where nothing annoying can follow me. Where I can't get right now because I've left my goddamn keys there.

This is the afternoon when my first waitress note is born:

I'M MAD!!! JUST MAD! I forgot my keys, and I know it doesn't sound like a big deal really, but when you're broke a simple absence of keys can easily drive you mad! I can't enter my home and my phone's dead, so I can't call the spare key guardians. I don't even have enough cash for a soda in the café. As if all that wasn't bad enough already, as I stood there by the useless doorbell, I felt I needed to take a dump. That led to one of those number two stories that a lady should never share...

After a sweaty experience of searching for a suitably hidden place and available resources, I decided to go to the café anyway. (I didn't do the number two there because I'd rather do my number two outside than in a public restroom. It's one of my greatest fears in life!) So I'm drinking tea now, because it's the cheapest thing on the menu, and there's at least an hour left before someone from my family gets home. I'm as poor as a church mouse. No. A church mouse is wealthier – it has a view of the church donation box, and I don't even have that.

Enough of this money situation! My no-money situation, that is! I REFUSE to be someone who drinks herbal tea in cafés on the hottest of days. I refuse to be someone who asks the waiter for a pen and paper so I can write about how desperate I am... I'm getting a job tomorrow!

Tomorrow I'm still too messed up. The day after, however, I actually start searching.

I remember struggling to find a part-time job after I finished high school. As so often happens, my initial efforts resulted in attending a meeting of some cult-like wellness company. Here's what happens: you're lured in by an ad promising that you'll "work as an independent consultant in the world's fastest growing industry; prime income opportunities for a flexible schedule and a once-in-a-lifetime chance to improve your health and the health of your family with our products." You meet the requirements, so you go to an interview and then to one of their private gatherings. They treat you to a free bottle of mineral water and a free screening of a couple of life-changing videos. Members of the cult may even come out to share in person how the wellness industry turned their once-sick life into a happy, healthy fairy tale. Before and after stories. All you need to do is buy – and then start selling – a number of miraculous dietary supplements worth about double the average monthly salary, an amount you surely don't have. But who cares about your two salaries when they can provide you with water from the Fountain of Youth?

"Dear guests! Is there anybody in this room who can stand up and claim: 'Yes, I am perfectly content with every single aspect of my life!'?" the cult's host asked. It was a rhetorical question but I didn't get that in time.

"I'm perfectly content with all aspects of my life!" I said, too proudly and too loudly.

Classic me, doing the most inappropriate thing at the most inappropriate moment. My answer couldn't have been more wrong. The sleek-haired dick pulled on a sleek smile and diligently pointed out exactly what was wrong with my life.

"Is that acne I see on your face, young lady? If you start using our high-quality products, your acne will become an unpleasant memory in no time, and your beauty-meter will go up by at least one point! Together with a whole lot of other meters too!"

Congratulations, Mr. Sleek-Wellness! You've got your strategy right, absolutely – telling an upbeat young person that she's got pimples. Keep up the good work!

Which he did.

"Do you want to join our harmonious team and improve your life by buying a package of… bla-bla-bla … at a promotional price of –"

"I don't."

Then I left.

Looking for a job hasn't changed much. Same old shit. A ten-minute scroll through the ads is enough to send my enthusiasm to the electric chair. I didn't go to Hogwarts and I can't morph into a witch who's both outrageously young and outrageously experienced at the same time. I only meet the requirements for an office assistant but my CV doesn't include any desire to work 9 to 5 all year long, wearing a suit, serving coffee to people in suits more expensive than mine…

I'd better go out with Venus and Annie!

So easy. We hit the karaoke bar again, and guess what! Just like that, out of the blue, I'm offered a job. The waiter has vanished along with the bar's revenue from the last few days, and Friday and Saturday are coming – too many customers to handle without service. It's an emergency, and we've become regulars because of Tino, so the staff trusts me. They ask me to substitute although I don't have any experience. I'll give it a try this weekend and then we'll decide if I'm to keep the job.

I keep the job.

"Nice, Alice! This job at the bar is a great opportunity for you to evolve as a writer."

I've been penning down my life experience for many weeks now. Annie keeps coming up with new incentives to keep me writing and writing and writing. She really has a way of making everything seem truly inspiring.

"You wanna be a really good writer? Then move on from the stage of forever debating what kind of person you are. You need to pay more attention to how other people are, and interacting with the customers at The Mockingbird is just the thing you need."

"You're probably the only one who thinks that…"

Ever since I started working at the bar, my family has been broadcasting one and the same chant: "You're wasting your potential in that place! Get a real job!" It has become a constant, everyday rant. Whenever I crash at Venus's – which happens a lot these days – my parents still call to check up on me and reiterate the same all-familiar diatribe.

"A waitress! You idiot!" My dad, foaming at the mouth.

"Please, Alice!" My mom, damp at the eyes. "By all means, you must give up this job! You always come home so late at night, it's not right, you're not getting enough sleep! We'll help you out until you finish university."

"University! What university? She's an idiot! She doesn't go to university anymore!"

Most of my friends also disapprove of my decision to work as a waitress. I don't care; we've become strangers anyway. Disconnected. They seem to have found their way, consistently devoted to whatever real jobs they discovered. No one knows about Venus or Annie. And all I know is that I need more time. I need to experience more worlds before I reconsider my friendships.

"You're not a flower that would thrive in an office environment, Alice," Annie's pep talk is still on. "Do you have fun while working at the bar? Then you're not wasting any potential."

"Oh Annie, you always make it sound like life itself is a waitress who'll bring me whatever I want!"

"Life's buffet-style, baby, you don't need a waitress. Just serve yourself whatever you want!"

She's a weird combination of a mischievous cheerleader and a stern career counselor.

"You're wasting your potential in that place!" my family keeps chanting, but my heart says Annie is right. Every occupation, regardless of its "intellectual" level, brings you some new knowledge. I don't want to be stuck in the routine washing machine of an office job. I don't want detergent all over my dreams. I must try out as many different jobs as possible in this life.

My lifeguard training taught me that I need to secure my own safety first, and only then go on to save people's lives. A valuable lesson. And another one that I learned during the short period when I worked as a teacher: clumsily-made Christmas cards with the word "thank you" misspelled can make you feel like someone capable of changing the world.

What can I learn from a bar job?

All Kinds of Hatters

Bartender claims that after so many years of working in bars he has people all figured out. "There's a finite list of personality types, Alice, and it's not so hard to learn to distinguish them. Everyone is a certain character from *Tom and Jerry*, you know."

Men's love for cartoons is endearing. Still, I don't like how Bartender brushes everyone under the rug of predefined categories.

A slow night at The Mockingbird. A tap-dancing silhouette materializes in the doorway. Tino, who else? Being a mere cartoon character isn't enough for him – he has to go and take over the joint with his trademark over-the-top animation.

"Tino in da house, yo!" Like he owns the place. He makes other things his own too: the casual lean against the bar, the right to make me laugh until I cry. But he doesn't own me. I know better than to fully trust someone that confident. "Get me a beer with a slice of lemon, would you, hon, 'cause it's been a hell of a cataclysm today! We wasted some granny's kitty and it was pretty hectic!"

This is the beginning of a surreal story that I'll try to reproduce here. Mind that I can in no way match the original narrator's acting or speaking skills. Ladies and gentlemen, I give you Tino. The scriptwriter. The performer. The director of most-unlikely scenarios. Always proudly emphasizes that he studies in the national film academy, and his very life is a busy movie studio too. Soap operas, comedies, neo-noir and all – having him around feels like attending a film festival. You can never be sure if Tino's adventures actually happened, but he recounts them with shameless talent, making you inevitably listen, gasp and chuckle along. What follows here barely scratches the surface of Tino's mastery.

The Cat

As usual, the main character of the story is Tino himself. In addition to his occupation as a troubadour and his ongoing studies to be an actor, he also works at the airport, something to do with loading luggage. It's another one of Tino's many curious traits – the range of totally random and bizarre jobs he does, or has done at some point in his short, but extra-exciting life.

So it's another day at the airport. An old lady comes up, carrying a cat in a cage. Lady's destination of travel remains unknown to us, but surely Cat is expected to arrive there too. Then, however, as our guy Tino and an anonymous coworker transport Cat to the cargo hold...

"It just so happened that Cat died. I mean, literally. Cat keels over and the next moment all we know is it's dead. Like, way dead. Thing is, it was a pretty ancient cat to begin with, I swear to God!" pleads Tino.

Instead of reporting the accident, he comes up with a plan.

"I tell my buddy, 'Hang on, how about we just swap the thing? You know? There's plenty of well-fed, resilient cats hanging around the airport restaurants.' I'm like, 'Here's what we gonna do, man. We swap the cat. Then we're golden,' and my boy's right on."

After some hilarious mishaps that I won't even attempt to describe here, the guys finally manage to capture one of the elusive restaurant cats. The situation is not quite perfect though.

"Well, the colors didn't really match, you know. Dead Cat was more of a gray color, and we got us a ginger one... And it wasn't a grown-up cat, 'twas a little kitten... But we thought about it, okay? We figured it'd be nice to give Lady a youngster, all right, mortality-wise, and all! So Lady has a new cat now. No harm done."

There's no known record of the old lady's reaction upon seeing her transformed cat.

I keep delivering beer with lemon to Tino. He keeps delivering sketches. After imparting a final cliffhanger, he leaves the bar. Once Tino's gone, it's Bartender's turn in the spotlight.

"You're aware that your friend is a mythomaniac, right?"

I shrug an *I don't know what you're talking about* shrug.

"A *mythomaniac*, Alice! People like him have mythomania. They're maniac liars. Saying all kinds of crazy stuff, dicking people around. Nothing about him is true. I'm pretty sure he even incorporates movie lines into his speeches."

I'm quick to change the subject. Tino is fun and I think only someone with no imagination whatsoever can judge him that hard. Granted, I myself have noticed certain discrepancies in his stories, but what's the harm there? If anything, they make life seem more vibrant and humorous.

Another slow night, only Bartender and I. My autopilot is off. My chit-chat autopilot, you know? I turn it on with most people because they tend to bore me quickly. My head is well-trained to climb and descend, turn left or right, depending on whether I'm nodding yes or shaking no, without the conscious participation of my brain. People never realize that I'm spacing out. Or maybe they don't care. Maybe they just want to spill their guts.

I don't do any of this with Bartender. It's funny how I feel both agitated and intrigued by his constant need to label everyone. I've heard him express negative opinions about Roma people, Jewish people, people from all around the globe, short people, overweight people, women, people who enjoy a certain type of music, and people who don't enjoy music at all… His remarks are outrageous, but at the same time he has a way of making things sound logical and not really malicious.

Tonight I'm completely absorbed in his stories about The Mockingbird's past. Until a couple of months ago, it wasn't a karaoke venue. The place, long known as ENTRANCE, was historically the first gay bar above ground in town.

"Back in the early 2000s when I first started bartending, all the gay hangouts around here were literally underground. So we decided to create a new bar for the gay community, with windows and all. It took them some time to get used to the light – at first they only wanted the booths in the back, but eventually made their way up to the windows. And let me tell you, they absolutely loved it. It was like a mass coming-out!"

Warm springs of excitement and pride in my heart. I'm part of a revolutionary open-minded place!

"For a damn long time, we were rated as the trendiest queer spot in town. Always packed, big time. The line of folks waiting to get in stretched all the way to the boulevard. We held a drag show once a month too, and it was lit! The night of the show was the only chance for guys to come in cross-dressed 'cause on regular nights we didn't let men in women's clothes in, you know?"

"Wait… What? Don't you think people should have the right to dress how they want?" The disappointment. I'm not part of a revolutionary open-minded place after all.

"Yeah, I'll tell you what… It was a bit complicated. Now the stars of the show, the drag queens, they were cool. But you've seen the cross-dressing hookers on the street around here? We didn't want the hookers. We also had some high-end customers and regulars who didn't want the hookers around either. The hookers would come straight over after work to earn another ten bucks or so in the restrooms. It wasn't exactly good for business, you catch my drift? So we came up with this face-control policy, brought in a bouncer to weed out the guys in drag. It was really just to keep the hookers away, that was the point. Anyway, they found a way around it. After work they changed into men's clothes in the building next door. Once in the bar, they'd hit the restrooms again. Imagine that!"

"Well, it does sound a bit complicated, but I still don't think telling people what to wear was an okay solution."

He sighs. I'm an ignorant little girl and he's the adult who has to explain the obvious.

"Trust me, Alice, handling a queer venue is a tougher job than you'd think!"

He goes on to elaborate that on the one hand, there were the customers who hated having hookers around, but on the other hand, they also resented the bar's attempts to keep them out. Several guys filed claims of discrimination. Queer people, Bartender says, sometimes cling to the topic of discrimination even when it's completely out of place. Like once some fellow asked for agave syrup. What bar keeps agave syrup in stock? Bartender replied that the closest thing they had was tequila, and the guy allegedly said he was going to press charges because Bartender was disrespectful to him because he was gay.

"How does that even make sense?" Bartender's speaking so loud right now. Apparently the whole thing really got to him. "So now all of a sudden I can't even crack a regular joke without someone getting offended! Like the whole world has to revolve around their feelings. What does tequila have to do with being gay? Talk about reverse discrimination, right? Anyway, there's also too much gossiping and way too much intrigue in gay hangouts. Eventually the management had enough and decided to turn the place into a karaoke bar instead."

I'm chugging straight whiskey to help me process the conversation.

"Wow! I don't even know what to say right now. Like, you're stereotyping everything so freely!"

I haven't forgotten the prevalent behaviors I discovered after entering certain societies and having the opportunity to actually observe what was going on there. Still, Bartender seems to be taking it too far.

"Ah, yeah," another sigh on his part. He's such a nuisance sometimes. "The pure-hearted, anti-stereotype advocate, aren't you, Alice? It's so easy, preaching about how to get along with people you've never personally interacted with. Do you even have friends who are gay?"

When I was a kid, there was a guy who sold ice cream in the park, a perpetual white cap on his head. Always the same white cap, every summer. The White Hatter, we called him. I found the way he moved his hands very unusual, but someone told me that was how gay men usually moved their hands. It was the first time I consciously registered someone as gay and I just took it as a fact – so he likes guys, whatever, it's his business. He's a person just like everyone else.

One of my friends on the block used to have a mermaid Barbie. He liked playing jump rope with the girls; whenever he had to participate in superhero games with the boys, he always insisted on being Catwoman. Again, I just took it as a fact – so he feels more like a girl, whatever, it's his business. He's a kid just like the others. I didn't feel anything in particular when he came out years later.

That's about it. I've never really poked my nose into who people like to go to bed with, or how they identify themselves. None of my business.

"I've only got one friend who's gay, but I think that's just because I don't really know a lot of gay people," I say somewhat defensively.

"Oh, I bet you know a lot but you haven't even noticed. Girl, you're probably both the smartest and the most oblivious person I've ever met! And you say you want to write books! How the hell are you gonna write about people when you don't know jack about psychology?"

That gets me fired up.

"So now I'm a clueless dumbass just because I don't label everybody all the time?"

"Look, I didn't mean to offend you, okay?" His hazel eyes also on fire, although it's a different fire than mine. A tender, amused fire, like when someone you really like acts ridiculous but you're not mad at them. Light-colored eyes are too cold. Dark eyes – too hot. Bartender's hazel is the perfect temperature to give me the feeling of being genuinely admired, even when the way he speaks is too patronizing for my taste. "Look, Alice, I'm not telling you to hate anyone. I'm just saying you could like people in a more informed way, sort of. You need to be more aware of the tendencies of different groups of people. I mean, come on, what are you going to write about otherwise? Books where the characters just do what you want them to do, not following any of the psychological mechanisms that are at play in real life? If you want to write books that feel real, you need to pay attention to the way people actually behave. Otherwise, your characters are going to come off as cardboard cutouts. Trust me, readers can tell when you're faking it. So – Jesus! – try to open your eyes a little wider, would you?"

Would you shut up if I kissed you? The idea tiptoes across my mind. But no. Ending this argument with a kiss would be a pretty unfeminist thing to do. I steam on instead.

"I'm all about learning the mechanisms at play. That's why I'm here, actually. It's just that the way you categorize people with just a wave of your hand makes it seem like you don't see them as unique individuals. And you're not tolerant at all!"

The hazel fire glows on. Still no trace of anger.

"Oh, you just don't get it. Sorting people into groups and recognizing their quirks isn't being intolerant, it's being smart. It's called being observant and learning from experience so you don't make the same mistakes over and over again. I have lots of gay friends and I love them just the way they are, quirks and all. And if I were any good at writing, knowing these little eccentricities would allow me to create relatable gay characters. So while it's true that some ignorant assholes out there may harass people who are different, that doesn't mean we can't be honest about the common traits we observe."

He has a point. He really does pay attention to the details and connects them to form the big picture. Skills I'm desperate for.

Antoine, 29, trans. Single. One of our most flamboyant regulars, inherited from the ENTRANCE days. She loves singing oldies with an amalgam of ridicule and excruciating pathos. Bartender told me that in the ENTRANCE era Antoine was the brightest star in the drag show. She used to call herself "Antonella," but then discarded that alter ego for reasons unknown. All that's left of her feminine attire is black eyeliner. Still, Antoine says I'm already her friend, and her friends should refer to her as "she." People who aren't her friends can't do that. She'll beat the shit out of them if they do.

There's something really awe-inspiring about her — she projects dignity and confidence, as if past insults never affected her. Antoine's favorite pastime is hitting on Tino and I'm pretty sure he loves it. A great trigger for explosive performances of the oh-horror-a-drag-queen-wants-to-get-me-laid type.

"Antoine, I need to explore the gay scene. Can you show me around?"

My approach in asking for favors has never been too imaginative. But then again, I dated George, remember. I've come to discover that the cleanest way to get what you want is to unapologetically ask for it. Antoine seems totally fine with my strategy.

"Anything your heart desires, my dear! Shall we commence this evening?"

"Sure."

And so we commence. The mission continues for the next month or so. Antoine takes her role as tour guide to heart. Waits for me to finish my shift, then shows me new haunts every week. Indeed, most of them are underground. Small doors barely noticeable among the shopfronts. Pictures of naked men on the walls. A lot of Madonna on the playlists. I'm completely mesmerized by this one bar – it's on the ground level, but underneath is an intricate labyrinth of corridors and rooms.

"And these are the premises for snorting and sex!" my tour guide announces. "But I must caution you, princess, venturing beyond this point may lead to rather spiritual encounters."

Antoine knows everyone and commands a lot of respect. We usually get free drinks and sometimes even free Annie, thanks to her connections. Whenever she spots a prominent figure in the LGBTQ+ community, she instantly fills me in on their backstory and then introduces me to them. I now know who has a criminal record, who's been in street fights, who's famous for their drag performances, who's been a mistress in the mafia circles, and who's engaged in sex work. I know who's dated who and who's cheated on whom.

"Haha, well maybe Bartender is right about something. You just love gossiping!" I giggle upon yet another serving of spicy information.

"You bet!" Antoine giggles in response. "Rest assured, you can always trust me to talk smack about people behind their backs. But you know what else, darling? You can also rely on me to be brutally frank and tell you what I really think directly to your face. Now that could prove quite useful, couldn't it? Besides, I talk shit about myself all the time too."

We're walking arm in arm through the night, searching for Boro. It's winter again. Early morning, still dark. The undefined, milky dark of starless nights. With my current lifestyle this darkness is often all I get to see for days. I go to bed in the morning, just before dawn, and when I wake up, the murk is already creeping in outside. I don't like it, but if anything, nightlife keeps me from slipping into another trap of depression.

"Bartender says I must learn how to *sort* people. With my aspiration to be a writer and all, you know? But the way it sounds! *Sort* people, like they're not unique pieces of art. Like they're just socks and underwear that need to go in their respective drawers."

"Bartender is right," Antoine pats my hand. "You should listen to Bartender. And he's very fond of you as well. The way he looks at you, I'd say he's in love!"

I laugh the hint off. I've been aware of Bartender's constant eyes on me ever since I first went to The Mockingbird. And the thing is, I constantly check if they're still on me too. Our interest in each other is palpable. Bartender's feelings though, and mine in return, are among the confusing things

I'll get around to later. Surprisingly, Antoine doesn't dwell on the subject either. She rattles on about psychology, how its very existence as a science and everything implies that a person is not completely unique and they can be categorized. How bartenders and taxi drivers are the best psychologists, and how working in a bar gives you much more psychological knowledge than university classes on the subject could offer.

"So what are we saying here, really?" I ask once we find Boro and I can finally channel my thoughts into clear sentences. "All these years I've been taught how great diversity is, that I must embrace diversity – which I do! – but now suddenly I'm supposed to admit that diversity is overrated? That we're not actually that diverse? When I got this job, I thought I was supposed to observe people's uniqueness, and now it seems I'm supposed to observe their sameness?"

"Well, my dear, at every party there's always someone who's different enough from the others that they withdraw and put on some music. But are they really that different? Allow me to reiterate: there's someone like that at *every* party."

It's been snowing. Feels as if we're walking on a movie set – snow always has this effect on me. Everything grows eerie and quiet. You can hear everyone's footsteps. Spoken words sound profoundly intense.

"We're peculiar creatures, princess. One-winged, one-armed. The wing urges us to strive up for the sky, for perfection, distinctiveness, outrageous ideals! Divine wisdom! But we can't exactly soar with the eagles, having just one wing, can we? Our one arm renders us all too human. And an arm isn't necessarily a bad thing. Not in the least. Arms, with their hands, itch to make things, be practical. However, it's no easy task, fashioning things with just one arm. The wing doesn't help much in that regard. So that's our vicious cycle. Nothing's easy for us, yet the most fascinating results can arise in this clash between the wing and the arm."

I imagine Antoine making a snow angel. She'd make the most beautiful one-winged, one-armed angel. I examine the ground. It's too clean with all the garbage carpeted under the snow, but I'd rather see the garbage than walk on it unaware.

"Fine then. I'll try to sort people out." A declaration as I kiss Antoine goodnight before disappearing into my building. Everything in life happens for a reason, and just like Annie said, this could give great Meaning to my job as a waitress.

"We're all characters from *Tom and Jerry*." It still escapes me what Bartender means by this. He's way ahead of me when it comes to categorizing. He starts with the shoes. According to his theory, the style and the condition of one's shoes can instantly reveal the owner's most noteworthy features. Then his eyes move up to the hands. "By the marks on their hands, you can tell who's hiding a wedding ring in their pocket, who has attempted suicide by slitting their wrists, and who has bitten their nails because they were anxious. Sometimes you can even tell people's profession with one look at their hands."

These abilities don't rub off on me. Bartender has pink laces on his Vans and I can't make anything of this fact. Pink laces don't match his hardcore appearance at all. I asked him about it once, but he didn't answer; stayed silent for the rest of the evening. I don't think I'll ever pick up on the famous intuition which allows you to guess what strangers will drink either. But I find it entertaining to build my own theories.

First, I sort people's faces. It helps me to remember them, because I struggle with that too. I think everyone resembles either a bird, or a particular breed of dog. Even if your nose doesn't look like a beak, you can still resemble a bird. Many people simply have something bird-like in their faces. Venus is a bird, so exquisite and frail and in her own world.

Tino is a Jack Russell – witty-faced, over-energetic, compact yet capable of huge havoc.

Dealers, unlike everyone else, always look like cats to me. They might be skinny, they might be fat, indoor cats or strays, but they're all cats just the same.

Once I'm done with facial taxonomy, I move on to drawing conclusions about the different types of personalities behind the dog, cat or bird facades. Friday nights are the most revealing in this respect. On a Friday night The Mockingbird is the most crowded, people are the most prone to opening up, and I'm the most prone to chatting eagerly with them. Because Friday night is the first day of the week when I'm with Annie; I itch to talk, ponder and write. As I work, I scribble down on the back of my waitress notes whatever little thoughts I have. Longer contemplations are left for after work, when I'm lying in bed with Annie.

Pieces of paper... So many loose pieces of paper, bearing loose thoughts on my loose conversations with loose people...

Some people shine. They're beautiful. They might not even be beautiful in the conventional sense, but when they speak, when they laugh, when you look at them ... they shine so brilliantly that it takes your breath away and blinds you to all imperfections.

Other people seem to be long-extinguished.

"What about me? Which character of *Tom and Jerry* am I?"

"Heh, Alice, that's easy! You're the little diaper-wearing mouse that always acts audacious and puts on airs, but is actually clumsy and vulnerable. You know, the little gray mouse who sometimes speaks French."

What really gets on my nerves are people who think they're geniuses just because they watch the *Discovery Channel*. Suddenly they're experts, acting like they know everything. The only truth in the universe is what they saw in some documentary or what they read in an article. And you see, Alice, you can't question their sources! These guys can spew out nonsense until you find yourself desperately looking for the reset button somewhere on their forehead. Stop wasting your time. There'll never be a reset button.

The people-with-blinders category includes individuals who give others a certain name and refuse to make the effort to remember how they're actually called. I'm sure you know someone like this. Someone who decides that a *Nicole* is named *Michelle* and they insist on calling her that even after you've corrected them thousands of times. Stop wasting your time. They won't ever acknowledge that they might be wrong. Like seriously, they can't even respect a person's name, how can you argue with someone like that?

People who always wear black. Give them a chance. A sunny personality could emerge from under the layers of darkness.

Girls who dress in pink from head to toe, speak louder than you like, overshare about their sex lives. Give them a chance. It might turn out they're not as shallow as they seem at the first few glances.

The miniature pinschers. Always yapping at people when it's obvious their yapping's only for show, and they'd secretly piss in your shoe rather than tell you straight to your face they don't like you.

"Man! That chick is ugly!"

One of our regulars, a miniature pinscher of thirty-something. Constantly on the search for a woman to start a family with. He will come and sit at the bar, turn on his "future-mother-of-my-children" radar and size up all the girls. Make comments about the looks of every female around. Once I asked him if it wasn't too superficial to choose a wife based solely on her appearance. He said it was important to him that his kids were good-looking, so his future wife's genetics were of the utmost significance.

"But she's not ugly!" I say.

"Whatever, the way she drinks is disgusting!"

The girl comes to get a drink from the bar. Stumbles over the pinscher's wide grin.

In a bar, there's too much attention on how people look. Never before have I been more aware of having a butt. Tonight I'm particularly aware of it because I was stupid enough to come to work in heels. The higher the heels, the more exposed, naked and butt-slapped I feel... Maybe because my intimate parts are raised a few centimeters closer to everyone's gaze? And no one seems to care to pretend not to be looking. One guy even tried to be all touchy-touchy, but Bartender saw him and kicked him out. The prick slurred that I was "dressed to provoke," as if that somehow justified his behavior. It's just unbelievable that right here in this day and age, some people still don't understand that they have no right to touch others without their consent, even if they're in their birthday suits.

The experience really shakes me up. I don't want this kind of attention, and yet I want this kind of attention. Part of me seems to like it, even feeds on it, but at the same time I hate to be appreciated solely for my looks. The way I look is not a personal achievement; it's nothing to be proud of. I used to know that, but now I'm not so sure. On some deep level, I feel like society has somehow convinced me that my beauty gives me worth.

In front of the mirror back home, I decide to cut my hair short.

"Makes a good statement, I think!"

Next thing I know, I'm trying out different ways to style my short hair in the cutest possible way.

Then it's evening again. I'm resolved to just throw on some sneakers and a hoodie for work, but then I find myself carefully curating the best hoodie to go with my hair and the best sneakers to go with my hoodie.

So much for my statements.

A one-winged, one-armed creature I am.

I keep classifying and writing.

People who are only here for the stage. We have a lot of acting students coming in and it's no wonder. A karaoke bar means a stage, an audience and applause.

Actors around here wear scarves, or suspenders, or Converse (usually red). Or all three at once. They're a compelling guild, no doubt, only you can never predict when they'll switch from comedy to dangerous drama. They've read so much Shakespeare that you can't question their vast education even if they've never read anything else. They tend to consider themselves much *artsier* than the rest of us mortal people, which is also quite irritating.

In general there's this pretentious type of person – not only amongst actors – who goes to extremes to show how sophisticated their taste in art is. They throw around the words "too commercial" with abandon to emphasize how they're not part of the masses. In their language, "commercial" is always synonymous with "total crap." But I think there are two kinds of commercial art. There's the overhyped kind that's molded to fit what the masses consume, and then there's the kind of art that's simply so powerful that it leads to mass consumption. If you truly are such an interesting person, you'll find your own special way to appreciate it.

At The Mockingbird, we also have a genuine vocalist named Chaya. A cruise ship singer who dresses like a peacock and sings like a nightingale. She comes to our place in between cruises and graces us with her off-duty performances. However, Chaya's totally unknown outside the cruise ships and the karaoke bar. Her dream is to change this, but years have gone by without any luck. Everyone wonders why that is. The talent is there, she's charming and friendly, she seems to have everything she needs.

And it's not just Chaya – I'm surprised by the high number of people who sing notably better than many world-famous vocalists. Why don't they succeed? After keenly surveying these karaoke stars, I'm beginning to suspect there's a certain quality to success that we don't have a word for. You know the feeling you get when you make someone cry? You feel bad for hurting them, but there's also something like satisfaction creeping in, as if you get proof that you matter in this world because someone is shedding tears for you. We don't have a word for this weird sadism, yet we all know what it feels like. So it's the same with the special quality I've detected; it can't be called simply charisma, or talent, originality, luck, ambition, dedication, the courage to fight for your dreams. You could possess all of these undoubtedly nice traits, and still fall short of achieving your aspirations.

The quality that has no name is the exceptional ability to *truly* make your dreams come true.

Some people just do it. Others will never learn how.

The good news is that you can be happy even if you don't make your dreams come true, only this kind of happiness requires special skills too.

"Happiness suits you."
"Happiness suits everyone."
"Not in my experience."

Conversations about love.
"When do you think people's feelings are most truthful? When opposites attract, or when two souls are kindred?"
"Depends on whether or not we like ourselves. The people we fall in love with possess traits we admire. We sometimes admire certain traits secretly, but anyway, if I like myself as I am, I'll choose a man who's similar to me. But if I've wanted to be someone else my whole life, I wouldn't fall for a person like me. I'd be attracted to my opposite."

"Do tell me about Alice. Are you two hitting it off well?"
"Oh yeah, she's great to work with."
"Okay?"
"I know what you're after, Antoine, but there's nothing like that. There's no romance going on here. She's hot all right. And smart. Not very mature though. More of a pain in the ass, and a bit promiscuous too."
"Huh. So you want it all, do you?"
"I'll have it all. After she figures herself out."
"Oops… I think she just overheard us."
"Good. Now she knows what to do."

"How about you start looking for a real job already? By sticking with this bar gig, you're allowing life to slip through your fingers."

"I am. But fingertips are the most sensitive part of the body. Which means that this is the best way to feel life."

"Sis?! Why didn't you say you were coming? We're all booked at this point."

"Whatever. I don't want to sit anyway."

"Are you crying? What's wrong?"

"I hit Eddie last night."

"Oh. That's bad. Did he break up with you?"

"No, I think we're good now. But I *hit* him, Alice! You of all people know what this means. I've always sworn that I'd never be like Mom and Dad, that watching them fight was the most gruesome thing ever, and now I just go ahead and do the same fucking shit!"

"Welcome to the club, baby! I always swore the same, yet as you know I had a history of hitting George back when we were together."

"But Eddie didn't do anything that bad. George had it coming."

"No one is supposed to have it coming, Sis. You either break up with a guy, or choose to tolerate his shit. Hitting him is the weakest solution, but obviously we learned to follow this pattern, although we thought we'd learned to hate it."

Everyone has their childhood sob story to excuse what they've become. The question is, are you the kind of person to live up to the excuse, or the kind of person to break the cycle? I really hope I'll get around to breaking the cycle of addiction and abuse, even if I'm not doing so great at the moment.

I analyze dozens and dozens of additional personality types. People who expect us to switch off the AC or turn down the volume only for them. People who won't even notice that the AC or the loud music bother them. Both species have their particular advantages and disadvantages.

People who seem to have come to this world specifically to express condolences. A very perplexing type.

The clown groups. Separated, their members act normal and can be serious to the extent of drab. But when they get together, they're guaranteed to leave you in stitches. The Mockingbird's clown group call themselves *The Power Rangers* and their signature act is a striptease choreographed to the tune of the *Itsy Bitsy Spider*.

The zodiac believers. It's disturbing how many people ask for your sign as soon as they meet you, and then every new bit of information "makes sense" or "is weird," depending on whether it fits your astrological description. Many claim they don't buy into this shit, absolutely not, God forbid! But in the end it turns out they do buy into it, at least a tiny bit. After all, haven't I noticed that Leos are always so arrogant?

When I don't have much to do and I'm just kind of hanging out at the bar, there's always some sociable patron who figures they should keep me unwanted company.

"I'm a Virgo."

"I don't believe in astrology," I answer with about an eighth of my mouth.

"Oh yeah, me neither. I don't buy into that nonsense at all!"

Three minutes later, same patron:

"Is the bartender a Gemini? He acts different every time I come in here. Sometimes he's super sweet, and other times he keeps to himself, sort of distant or whatever. The other day he was openly rude … textbook Gemini! It's as if there are two completely different people sharing the same body. And they never know what they want, either."

I thought you said you didn't care for astrology? I'm tempted to respond, but I don't want to prolong the conversation unnecessarily. Despite my tedious efforts, the conversation continues.

"What's your sign again?"

Well, if you insist, I'm an Alice. And I'd venture to guess that you are a You, but if you prefer to consider yourself a Virgo, that's fine. Perhaps you'd want to do some rough calculations though:

7-odd billion people / 12 astrological signs

≈ 600 million people

600 million people who have the same qualities, flaws and appetites as you; who are diagnosed with cancer and win the lottery on the same day that you're diagnosed with cancer and win the lottery; and all that just because their mothers gave birth on a certain date. 600 million people! Even more, if extraterrestrials have signs too.

"Capricorn," I reply in a monotone. I know better than to try to express my opinion.

Naturally, I'm instantly informed about the status of some of my 600 million sign-mates in my new buddy's life. Every single man I've had the pleasure or displeasure of meeting has been with at least one Capricorn woman. And she has invariably treated him in a terrible way. And I invariably have to hear all about it. Good thing I know how to nod along without paying attention.

Then there are the girls with a hippie vibe that Tino usually shows up with. They're all quite similar to one another, some of them sport dreadlocks. They speak and move about in some sort of enchantment, kind of dazed, as if they'd spent the last half hour in a scented-candle shop.

Recently, Tino and Venus finally decided to officially declare themselves a couple. She dyed her hair pink; a celebration of this important change in her life. Anyway, she still makes herself throw up every once in a while. Whenever she goes back to shutting herself away at home, Tino brings more of his hippie girls to the bar. Allegedly friends only. No benefits. Venus doesn't have it in her to confront him. Pretends she doesn't mind, but I know she does, oh yes she does, although her passive-aggressive remarks are really subtle. She's painfully jealous of the girls' slightly filthy yet pretty faces. And jealousy is a new thing for Venus. She's what I refer to as a Triple P in my notes. A Peaceful People Pleaser. Doesn't have the slightest idea how to deal with the maddening feeling of jealousy. Never shouts. But the noise she makes when she throws up sounds like shouting. The cuts on her thighs look like shouting.

She's started cutting herself lately.

I saw a girl cutting herself at the bar once too. Our lemon knife in hand, she stood in the middle of a group of people. Bartender kicked them all out when he realized what she was doing. The girl said cutting was trendy.

This is the most exciting part – discovering weird similarities between diverse personality types. Almost everyone that I've asked, even the most rational individuals, reckons they've seen an alien at least once in their lives. Or a UFO.

"You're a very strong person!" Use this phrase if you want to make someone instantly like you, or if you want to make them feel better – depending on whether you're the type who likes to be liked, or the type who likes it when others feel good. Anyway, all you have to do is say, "You're such a strong person!" with a serious enough expression, and even the weakest person will fall for it.

Confession:
I also saw a UFO once, but I prefer not to talk about it because people will think I'm crazy.

"You people always accuse each other of being selfish. Is selfishness really the worst trait a human can have?" Annie asks lazily.

Up until recently, her thing was to get me talking or writing about how amazing she was. Lately she's been backpedaling; maybe because she's increasingly losing her grandeur. She wants me to think of her presence as a given. No need for further discussion. We talk long about psychology instead – my new favorite topic.

"No, selfishness isn't inherently bad. No. It can be hugely powerful in a beautiful way. It urges you to look after yourself above all else and that way you don't bother other people, and you're well enough to look after them too. But only if you think it's reasonable to do so! You love yourself, thus setting an example both for others to love you, and for you to love them in return. Your trust lies in your conscience, not in those who try to manipulate it. You don't waste time constantly proving how good you are, but you do occasional good deeds when needed. Or at least you don't harm anyone. You're too focused on your own life to feel envious of others and stand in their way."

"So envy is the worst human trait then."

"I think so, yeah. Envy is inevitably a lose-lose situation. If you're miserable anyway, why let others' happiness bring you down even further? An envious person could be a really bad person because they focus on the desire to take something away from others instead of creating something for themselves."

"And what, in your opinion, defines a truly good person?"

"You know, Annie… As much as people annoy me at times, I believe that generally we're good. We rarely have mean intentions. Granted, our execution is often faulty, but I still think intentions count when evaluating what a person is like." My head is sandwiched between two pillows, eyes tightly shut. I badly want to go to sleep, but my brain won't stop running around. Swirling with Annie. "Anyway, if you insist on a precise answer about goodness, personally I have the most respect for people who don't feel entitled. Like, in a relationship, they make the effort to keep the fire blazing instead of just presuming that their partner won't cheat on them or that others won't show interest in their partner. These people can build a nice life even in the un-nicest country. They're not a common breed though," I sigh in conclusion. I'm too tired to think anymore. "What do you want me to write about next?"

"It'll come to you. Just keep on taking notes."

A Penguin and a Few Pebbles

When you find yourself in a new environment, the first things you tend to notice are the beautiful and the crazy. Once you get used to the crazy, you start feeling at home. You put your house slippers on, so to speak. If you leave for a while, the crazy will be patiently waiting to welcome you back. It's like old furniture – you barely pay attention to it, or you're annoyed with how worn out it looks, but if it happens to disappear, the feeling of home goes away with it. And then you have to get used to the place all over again.

I'm already familiar with the crazy population that inhabits the neighborhood of The Mockingbird. I'm home here. I have two favorite people:

A petite elderly woman. Always in her floral dressing gown by the dumpsters, rearranging their contents, shouting at me every time I take the garbage out. She's just put everything in order, she screams, can't I see that I'm making a mess again?

A middle-aged, willowy man. His speech is as educated as it is incoherent, but when someone attempts to make fun of him, he recognizes their mockery at once. "The falcons look on from above!" he says then. I think he's referring to God.

The elderly woman is a Pekingese. The middle-aged man, an Afghan Hound.

These types of crazy people – the obvious ones – can mislead you into thinking that everyone else is quite sane. But I don't think so. I kissed that delusion goodbye a long time ago. Rumor has it that one in five people on the planet is crazy. That's absolutely not true. Everyone on the planet is crazy. If we all went to have our brains examined, we'd all come away with at least one small diagnosis. I get to witness it with my own eyes. No matter how cool, entertaining or justifiably wild someone might seem when on stage at the bar, sooner or later they'll get off, come to me, and start talking. After work we'll go together for a drink somewhere else and... Well, they'll just prove to me that everyone's crazy.

This is my truth.

My hobby – collecting oddballs. No kidding. I expose myself to after-parties with all kinds of looneys, and my fascination with them borders on the scientific. I listen to all manner of weird stuff, eager to put it down in my collection album. It's good to keep such an album. After a while you come to realize that even people's craziness is alike; you learn to recognize the different types and you're not afraid of them anymore.

My most emotional experience with madness is my encounter with mythomania.

A fairly busy night. Tino shows up with a black eye. True to his theatrical code, he won't raise the subject of the puddle-colored bruise on his face. He sports a martyr-like expression, speaks in a subdued manner, diligently waiting for us to ask him what happened. True to his anti-Tino code, Bartender is silent. I can't keep it up.

"Tino! Did you get in a fight?"

"Oh, you mean the black eye?" A pause for a dramatic effect. "Don't sweat it, baby. I got my ass kicked by the cops, is all."

I jump up, horrified. He wouldn't make up something like this, would he? Of course he wouldn't.

"You got thrashed by the police?!"

"Oh, they jump everybody. Is cool, I ain't that special. They messed me up pretty good, but at least they finally cut me loose."

"Fuck, Tino! Cut the tough-guy act and tell me exactly what happened!"

"Here's the thing, Alice… You know when dudes go to prison?"

"I'm all ears."

"Dudes go to prison when they wish to be free!"

I grunt. Didn't I just ask to be spared the pathos?

"Ahaa, I see. You didn't do anything stupid, you just wished to be free?"

"Yup. Alice, hon, I wasn't stupid this time. I bombed a plane, that's it."

It takes me a few seconds to try to make sense of what he said. It doesn't make sense.

"Honestly, bombing a plane sounds incredibly stupid to me!"

"Hold up. Seems you don't know what a 'bomb' is," he laughs. Theatrical again. "S'not what you're thinking. I was just trying to make a dream come true."

The Bomb
(He Had a Dream)

It's not a story about clockwork destruction. It's about graffiti. Tino explains that there are two types of wall paintings: legals and bombs. The bombs are the real thing – rebellious pieces in forbidden locations.

"You must've seen the bombs on trains… I've done a lot of that, plenty of whole trains. But I dreamed of bombing a plane, making it count, you know! How awesome would that be? Just think about it. When I paint, I fly. And I was thinking, I want my art to fly too, bro, not to be dragged along on lame rails! Bombing a plane would make my art, like, fly right up in the sky. Think that was why I got a job at the airport in the first place. It sucked ass but I was biding my time. Pity it came right here in the middle of winter, you know!

Trust me, hon, it's not fun painting when it's below zero. The can sticks to your hand and it frigging hurts. But I put my stencil against the plane and start painting. Everything's maximum thrill, not givin' a care in the world about the pain and the cold! It was insane. I was so happy! Then those scumbag pigs nabbed me and ruined it all!"

Bartender shoots Tino with trick questions about the arrest procedure, trying to expose him. Tino's deft answers evade the traps; still, he's visibly jumpy. He soon offers a made-up-sounding excuse, and mumbles "Well, I'll bounce now," before sneaking away.

I'm used to the mood that Bartender reserves especially for Tino. A blend of ridicule and irritation. This time he's even more excited than usual.

"Hah! So predictable! An arrest story was the only piece missing from this clown's List of Lies!" The triumph in Bartender's "L"s makes me picture him crushing a fly he's been chasing the whole afternoon.

"And what would this List of Lies be?"

I pin a cigarette to my reluctant smile, bracing myself for another long session of criticizing Tino. The further Bartender goes into his List of Lies though, the more my inclination to take Tino's side points a finger at me, squealing with laughter.

Bartender says that he's known lots of people who later turned out to be mythomaniacs. They're quite the characters and crafty bastards, Bartender gives them that, but he's noticed absolute similarities in their ever-more-improbable stories. He's come up with a list of the generic fabrications that are supposedly employed by every compulsive liar out there.

Every self-respecting mythomaniac has traveled to unexpected places abroad, even lived there.

Tino meets requirement number one. He often brags about his travels across Europe to paint graffiti in different cities. He's also told us that as a child he lived somewhere in Africa with his family. There are three or four anecdotes about him playing with various dangerous creatures there.

Every self-respecting mythomaniac plays or has played an unusual sport. They're really good at it and they keep winning awards.

Tino does show his physical abilities off too. He claims to have won a silver medal in capoeira, only I can't remember if the championship was national or worldwide. He got silver because number one cheated; Tino deserved the gold, beyond any doubt.

Every self-respecting mythomaniac suffers from a serious illness, or they almost died of one in the past.

Yup. This was actually Tino's reason for quitting capoeira. He had an accident while training but he never feels like sharing details about it. He was paralyzed from the waist down and he couldn't walk for more than a year, that's all he'll say. Eventually a famous psychic healer got him back on his feet.

Every self-respecting mythomaniac works on a range of art projects that are yet to be released. The mythomaniac generously advises others on how to approach art, and also tends to present other people's art as their own.

Another item crossed off the list. Tino definitely likes to lecture me about my writing and he's shared a "secret" with me – besides his hundreds of other activities, he also likes to write. He still hasn't shown his stories to anyone... What about the graffiti then? Does he even do graffiti at all?

Every self-respecting mythomaniac is rich. They own companies, promise you jobs, yet keep relying on others to pay for their drinks.

Tino doesn't claim to be rich himself, but says that after his family returned from Africa his father suddenly became quite wealthy. He wants his son to learn to earn his own living, which is why he stopped giving Tino an allowance a long time ago.

Every self-respecting mythomaniac lies about having siblings and friends that don't exist, or the other way round – tries to hide the existence of real family members and friends.

I haven't delved into Tino's family tree, but there sure are things amiss in the stories he tells.

Every self-respecting mythomaniac tells so many military stories that their service seems to have lasted for at least ten years. Mythomaniacs from the younger generation who weren't conscripted claim that the uncanny stories they tell were experienced by their fathers or grandfathers.

Oh, the eventful military days of Tino's renowned father! His son's tales paint him as an irrefutable army hero. I, however, remember one story in particular: a gypsy guy tried to pilfer something from a military facility and Tino's father shot him dead because he knew he'd be granted leave for this "heroic act." Despicable.

Every self-respecting mythomaniac has overcome some addiction.

Another coincidence. The very first time we met, Tino told me he'd had serious drug issues. Also, he constantly announces how much he's had to drink each day. It's always a mystery to me why he's so eager to portray himself as a degenerate alcoholic.

Every self-respecting mythomaniac has had trouble with the police.

Look no further than his latest story about the bomb on the plane.

Every self-respecting mythomaniac makes up elaborate scenarios when they want to borrow money from someone. They can't simply admit they don't have the dough to get wasted tonight, no. They'd rather pretend they were robbed, or tell a sob story about needing the money to make their childhood dream come true, or casually mention a sick family member. Naturally, no self-respecting mythomaniac ever gives back what they borrowed. If the person who lent it dares complain to others about it, the mythomaniac will smoothly persuade everyone that they were actually the ones who lent the money, not the other way around.

I gave money to Tino only once. He told me he needed to pay for his Photoshop training by the end of the day. Later that week, I noticed that he owned a lighter with a casino logo on it.

Every self-respecting mythomaniac must claim that they've done everything you've done, and that they've got everything you've got. What they've got is actually more impressive. If you get a parakeet, they'll say they have a talking parrot who performs traditional dances. You've made up your mind to learn Spanish? The mythomaniac already speaks it to the point where they can read the original version of Don Quixote.

Sounds a lot like Tino as well.

Mythomaniacs don't think twice about playing with death. They're quite capable of lying about someone passing away.

I don't think Tino has gone this far yet, but who knows – I might've missed some macabre story. Or maybe the military thing with the murdered thief didn't happen after all? I really hope so.

The cherry on the List of Lies: every self-respecting mythomaniac would readily swear that at a certain stage in their life they traveled around with a circus.

"NO SHIT!" I choke. This last bit sounds too absurd, the most absurd part being that Tino did indeed tell me he'd toured with a circus for a while.

"When he was fifteen," I explain to Bartender. "Supposedly, he ran away from home and spent the whole summer helping tamers look after their wild animals – based on his childhood experiences in Africa. He even got to substitute for a lion trainer on stage once. It was a huge success, he said."

"Yeah, yeah, he told me the same story. That's what I mean – Tino embodies the whole List of Lies, top to bottom. Okay, I have to say that not every mythomaniac I know has a circus story. I added that one more for the fun of it."

"Nooo. No! I can't believe Tino's been pulling our legs all this time!"

I'm really disappointed. Not only has he lied about so many things, but on top of that, he isn't unique in doing so. Turns out he's just another mythomaniac, the type you can find anywhere. It's sick! The ultimate confirmation that even the most bizarre, fascinating or mean people we know are surprisingly similar to so many others out there.

"I can't even begin to fathom why the hell he'd lie about such nonsense!"

"Hah, Alice, people will always make a fool of you if you keep presuming that they should have coherent reasons for lying. More often than not, there isn't any logical explanation. Get that into your head and you'll make a huge step towards a wiser life."

"But what about Venus? Do you think he's lying to her too? About his feelings?"

"Pff… You bet! Actually that should go on the list too."

Every self-respecting mythomaniac cheats on several girls (or guys, depending on their preference) simultaneously. And these girls/guys were probably smitten by using one and the same strategy.

"Why didn't you tell me about the List before?"

"Don't say I didn't try, Alice! It's okay though. Mythomaniacs are expert psychologists. They know exactly what to say to come across as perfectly normal if you start to suspect them. Make you feel paranoid for doubting their word," Bartender is pretty bitter as he says this. "You'd better play cautious once you realize someone's a mythomaniac. No use running around warning your mutual friends. They usually believe the mythomaniac to the last minute, so if you act too hastily you risk coming across as the crazy person yourself. You've gotta wait for the lies to accumulate."

I fit right in the mold. I didn't want to believe how lousy Tino actually was, and I was annoyed by Bartender's distrust. No wonder he didn't share the List of Lies with me earlier. His ability to wait patiently is impressive. Nothing like me – I feel short of excitement in life if I don't rush into situations unprepared. Bartender has a completely different way of making things exciting for himself. Meticulously orchestrates the grand moments and then executes his plan with the finesse of a skilled illusionist.

"Mythomaniacs are sad people," I say before getting into the taxi after work.

"Sad, but not harmless. Especially if they look good."

I've never felt so much pain in Bartender's voice before.

Everyone lies. At least a little – to spare a nice person the bitter truth; to save themselves from work on a lazy day; to avoid public humiliation after doing something embarrassing. Sometimes we lie simply because we don't have it in us to say no. We've all done it and hell, it can be forgiven. But the trouble is that we all have at least one friend, coworker or family member who lies just for the sake of it. Think hard enough and you'll find out that in your world too, there's surely a mythomaniac who perfectly matches every criterion on the List. Someone who deceives others on such a regular basis that they don't have a real life anymore.

Can we forgive something like that?

Should I forgive Tino? Should I go on being nice? I know Venus won't bail on him just because someone said she should. People in love don't work like this. Won't I hurt her if I start being rude to Tino while they're still together?

I make up my mind to explain mythomania to her gently. After all, Tino is *her* boyfriend, so I'll let her decide how we should handle the guy.

Venus, being Venus, says exactly what I expect her to say:

"Perhaps what matters most about a person isn't whether they lie or not."

And: "Can we ever be sure that the truth is better than a beautiful lie?"

And also: "I don't fully believe him, but I want to believe. And it's not really that important what he feels for me – I'll still love him. One can love without being loved in return, you know, only it doesn't feel that nice. But it's not pointless because my love gives me Meaning. I'm sure it helps Tino and protects him on an energetic level."

Bartender is all about not letting people make a fool out of him. Venus is all about loving people. That makes her highly susceptible to being made a fool of, but she consciously chooses the risk over constant mistrust. It's a dignified attitude, I think, and I have no right to ruin it. I'll set aside my concerns about Tino for now.

My own romantic life is enough of a mess anyway.

"You will fall in love with someone with dark hair and dark eyes," the cleaning lady at The Mockingbird told me a while ago. Sometimes I buy her coffee and then she tells my fortune. The falling-in-love prediction came true. But why don't fortune-tellers ever specify that someone with dark hair and dark eyes will be mad too?

A man of art. What did I expect anyway? No matter how well you think you know people, you can still totally fall for the wrong guy. An affair with a man of art is a bucket-list must, sort of, but you must know better than to take him seriously.

Men of art are like plastic bags carried by the wind. I had a massive crush on the bag's wild, impetuous flight, but alas, it was meant to be a fleeting relationship. Yet again, I dreamed of having a beginning and an Eden, but it turned out to be just another beginning and an end.

My man of art had an impressive gaze. Dark and completely and utterly deep. I've only seen a gaze like that in street dogs. But he was no dog. If a stray dog likes you, it'll find a way to get on the bus with you, then follow you to the very entrance of your home, and if you open the door wide enough, it'll stay forever. Men of art don't do this. Aloof in their raw artistic sensibility, they can't just come down and share someone's everyday life.

"Sometimes I miss him, Venus. My man of art. Every now and then, I feel like shouting. 'I miss you, Plastic Bag!' But I don't shout. There's no point in shouting that you miss someone… If they were interested, they wouldn't be missing in the first place."

Venus and I are on the roof of my apartment building. I felt like pouring my heart out and I felt like doing it on the roof and nowhere else. In order to get here, we had to put up the wooden ladder that goes to the attic, climb through a small window, step out onto an even smaller ledge, remember to never look down, and then pull ourselves up onto the roof.

"Aren't you scared?" Venus had asked when we were about to climb through the window.

"Scared as hell. That's why I want to do it." Good enough to persuade her. She won't accept my resignation to the man-of-art situation though.

"I can't believe you're giving up so easily!" Tug-tug-tugging at the sleeve hems of her sweater. "You must fight for your love!"

Venus, the incurable romantic.

"Oh, come one! What does it even mean to fight for your love, Venus? Fighting FOR the person you love and fighting WITH the person you love are two different things. What am I supposed to do; dig my talons and beak into him? I like other parts of bird anatomy better. What about the wings? I don't want to stop him from using his wings. Let him fly without me, if that's what he needs!"

I'm overly satisfied with rebuffing her naive advice. Think I've developed a dislike for her childish faith in love. Perhaps I'm just bitter that my own faith has packed its bags and taken off.

"I'm strong enough to fight anything in this world for my love," I keep going. "But sometimes letting go requires more strength than fighting. I have that kind of strength too. It's about time we stopped *falling* in and out of love and started *flying* in and out of love instead."

A couple of nights later Venus shows up with a new necklace – a mediocre-looking pebble hanging from a gold chain. The pebble is plain and gray, one that you're likely to find anywhere.

"Tino told me he loved me!"

She's so happy. She's been fluttering for months, waiting to hear this. I smile and prompt her to recount the beautiful moment.

"Well, he didn't say the exact words, but he gave me this as a present," she caresses the stone with affection. "We went for a walk in the snow and he told me how penguins expressed their love. The male gave the female a pebble and if she accepted it, they'd stay together till the end of their lives. In joy and cold. Then he brushed the snow off a bench, spread out his jacket, sat me down there and told me to wait for him. And he came back with a pebble! I took it to a jeweler's to have it drilled and hung on a necklace."

After hearing the story, the pebble doesn't look mediocre any more. I choose to be happy for her and shove my distrust for Tino into the bowels of my mind.

Weeks later. I go out to have a smoke in front of the bar. Tino is sitting on the stairs to the entrance of the building next door with one of his numerous female friends. Obviously neither of them has seen me. But I can see and hear them clearer than I wish to.

"Do you know how the male penguins show their love to females?" he asks. She doesn't know. Luckily, he's there to tell her. "The penguin in love carefully picks, like, the smoothest, the finest, the most perfect pebble for the lady of his heart. He picks it up in his beak, all right, and wobbles back to her." Tino gets up for a quick personification of the cute penguin walk. "And if she wants them to stay together, she drops the pebble right into her nest. I'm saying, how cute is that? After they exchange this pebble of love, the two lovely birdies are gonna love each other till death."

"In joy
and cold,
baby."

The way he recites it! I'm positive that he used the exact same words when he told the story to Venus. It's time to reveal the gift now. He opens his fingers and there it is: a pebble. Only the festive music is missing. In joy and cold my ass! I'm boiling with rage. Ready to make a scene right here and now, but I have orders to take care of inside.

Tino returns to the bar a bit later, alone.

"You come to give someone else a pebble too? Dumb fuck!"

"Wait, what?! Hey, hey. What the hell, Alice?"

"I saw it all outside. Tonight you're coming with me to Venus, and I want you to explain just what kind of penguin you are!"

It only takes him a few seconds to collect himself and arrange his expression from, "I haven't the slightest clue" to an amused, "Hell, you're such a dumbass, Alice!"

"Je-e-e-ez!" He even smacks himself on the forehead. "I get it, I get it. You've got it all wrong, yo. Jesus. Lemme explain it to you…"

Tino's Version
The girl was his best friend. They hadn't seen each other for a while and he couldn't wait to tell her about his love for Venus. The scene that I witnessed outside was Tino reenacting to his best friend how he told Venus he loved her.

"You don't expect me to buy that, do you?"

An expression of infinite offense. Am I trying to ruin things between him and Venus on purpose? He makes a big show of being disappointed in me – he cares so much for both of us!

"Yo, let me tell you something," Tino's counter-attack gathers force. "You're obviously still stuck with Annie. She makes you see conspiracies everywhere, is all I can say! That's the thing. I'm just saying, you know."

His words hit home. Recently I myself have realized that I've grown to treat people with suspicion and contempt. As with everyone else in my life, Annie has started to show the cloven hoof. She doesn't come to us as generously as she used to back when the cats were trying to get us hooked. She finishes ever faster and her delightful influence is much fainter. She manipulates my moods according to her liking, often causing me to feel depressed instead of happy. The first few times I got scared because the depression she gives is much spookier than the one I had at home. But I quickly got the knack of it. As soon as the dark thoughts perch on me and start pecking, I isolate myself from people. I don't want some inner depressive monster of mine to get them weirded out, or to expose me. I face it alone, applying the same strategy that I use for nightmares that I don't want to wake up from because I'm curious to see how they'll end. I keep telling myself that they have nothing to do with reality, that they'll carry on for a while and then they'll just disappear.

Is it possible that Annie makes me exaggerate Tino's mythomania too? I don't buy the whole *best friend* trick, but still I won't make a fuss. Anyway, whatever I do, Mr. Honey-Mouth will bamboozle his way out and convince Venus of his innocence.

As I read *A Penguin and a Few Pebbles to Annie,* I try to keep my voice down because Venus is in her room on the other side of the wall. She's back to binging again and she's made her nest there. Clothes, stuffed animals and magazine clippings are strewn all over the floor, all over her queen-sized bed, and her king-sized melancholy. Shoes and jewelry too. Huge plastic bags of junk food. She won't put it in the fridge. Hides the supplies in her nest, which is okay because she doesn't give the products enough time to expire anyway. She eats in bed, hence the constellation of crumbs among the clothes, animals and magazine clippings. I expect her to go to the bathroom any minute now and stay there for ages gurgling and choking, because on top of everything, she doesn't throw up with ease. Her knuckles are always sore from trying. I wonder if Bartender knew about her condition as soon as he glimpsed her hands.

"We get so arrogant when we have someone to love us!" I add once I'm done reading. I want to distract Annie from my confession about being disappointed in her. "Isn't it crazy? People are eager to apologize to you a hundred times when they accidentally break a glass, but if they happen to break your heart – nah! – they'd rather make you apologize!"

Again, it seems Annie has no intention of commenting on her own appearance in my story. She's sitting across from me with a subtle smile, unfazed, eyes fixed on mine. As if no one criticized her, as if she hasn't noticed my new fear of her.

"Is your heart broken?" she asks.

"My heart has a broken hip." It sounded wittier in my head.

"It's okay, Alice. Things break, but the pieces are still there. And no matter what crises the media threatens you with, I've yet to hear of a glue shortage. You can glue everything back together."

"Well, I don't know if there's any will left in me to glue things back together," I frown. "Love! So much pain – pain that you cause, pain that you receive. Or rather, phantom pain that you inflict on yourself, or someone else tries to inflict on themselves… I think I've already run out of feelings."

She laughs in a way that makes pain seem petty and minor.

"The power to love is like toothpaste, Alice. You may think the tube is hopelessly empty, it may seem there's absolutely no chance of squeezing another drop out in the morning, and yet it turns out you can brush your teeth over and over again … all from the same tube."

Damn it! I realize I'm not ready to give up on her yet.

Film-Coated Pills

I've never been sensible enough to feel alive in the right way. But am I strong enough to recover from everything I've done wrong?

I can't tell for sure when I first started hearing the Voices. Summer exams were approaching and I decided to give them a try. I've barely shown up to any lectures for the last couple of semesters, but I want to graduate next year. Why not use Annie for concentration before we break up for good? I still work almost every night at the bar, but I try to get up reasonably early in the morning so I can catch up on my pile of unfinished essays. My relationship with Annie has changed. It's not just Fridays, Saturdays and Sundays with her anymore. It's an everyday thing. By the time most people are making their first coffee of the day, I cut my first line.

My essays are going well. My mental health – not so much. At some point I started having a sneaking suspicion that for some reason everyone was discussing me. I'd hear them, seated at the bar, making comments about my appearance, my behavior, even my thoughts. At times with approval, but largely with disdain. Some spoke about me having to stop seeing Annie, and I couldn't understand what was going on. *How come they know what I'm thinking about right now? Can't they see I can hear them? Why don't they keep it down? Why don't they mind their own business?* Several times I snapped at strangers that it wasn't okay to talk about me like that, as if I weren't there. All I got was startled looks. All I thought was how impertinent they were, pretending they didn't know what I meant.

Then I started hearing them at home too. The same Voices. I've come to notice that, strangely enough, it's not random people who speak; the Voices seem to belong to a particular threesome. And their sole topic is me. I'm never in on their jokes. I'm the joke.

At first I was anxious. *Are they continuously breaking in, or what?* But now I just assume that the Voices come either from down the street or from the neighbors. Day after day they make me jump, and day after day I jump to the same idiotic conclusions. *They're coming from down the street. No, from the neighbors. Remember that woman throwing up? Sound travels so easily in apartment buildings!*

Today I have to write an advertising strategy I've been putting off for months. Again, nothing creative comes to mind. Being much better at planning than actually doing the work, I remove the calendar from the wall to write down what I still need to do and how much time I have before exams. It suddenly strikes me that too many days have passed since the exclamation mark on the date of my last period. I count them. Far too many no-exclamation-mark days!

The shock. Man of Art must've gotten me pregnant! Only a stoned cow like me could've missed the symptoms! I've been dizzy, having weird food cravings, and I felt the usual pre-period cramps but then nothing came. The other day I even noticed something like dried white discharge on my nipples... The only thing missing is that smells don't make me sick, but maybe the opposite is also a symptom – recently I've lost my sense of smell altogether.

Panic. I start considering abortion. Annie's been a part of this baby's conception; I can't have it! Thinking about the intervention horrifies me. What if something goes wrong and I get punished with sterility forever? Against my will I start fantasizing about how I won't tell Man of Art anything, but he'll find out anyway and dash into the hospital and swear that he loves me and beg me to keep the child. *The child!* The Voices chime in. They want to make me see it as a baby full of life, and not a pea that can just be removed. They make me put my hand on my stomach. I'm certain I can feel the pulse of a little heart.

It was sent to you to be loved and protected from everything, and you plan to kill it!

Well done, Alice!

Well down!

I slam the window shut. Turn off the music that's been playing all morning; *Massive Attack* is hardly the best choice when you're trying to run away from some eerie voices. Still, they won't shut the fuck up. They're already calculating the baby's zodiac sign.

Probably Sagittarius. Like the father.

Or a Scorpio.

Loyal but controlling.

How do you feel about a little Scorpio, Alice?

I set off for the gynecologist. To hell with appointments. I have to be examined at once and my abortion has to be scheduled for tomorrow! The stairs turn to streets turn to boulevards, then a bus turns into a long white corridor (I hate long corridors), which turns into a crowd in front of the doctor's office. A largely pregnant crowd. I steal glances at the women, trying to read their stories. Hoping they can't read mine. The seconds turn to minutes and then to dull nothingness. When I finally talk to the doctor, my ears ring and I burst into tears. She gives me an ultrasound. No abortion needed. There's no pregnancy. Ovarian cyst, 40 millimeters; it will go away on its own.

"And the symptoms?" My voice is hardly more than a whisper.

She lets out a weary sigh.

"When women get it into their heads that they're pregnant, they can find all sorts of symptoms. You just need to see a breast specialist about the nipple discharge, although I doubt there's anything to worry about."

Before I know it I'm back in front of my building. My thoughts chase one another wildly, my mood a worn-out mixture of relief and exaltation that I don't have to kill any babies after all. It's warm – the kind of warmth on an early May day that smells like memories. Only I can't smell anything.

I don't feel like shutting myself back in the apartment, so I decide to climb up to the roof. Surprisingly, I don't fall in the process. The Voices follow me though.

She's not pregnant, not this time. But if she doesn't get rid of Annie...

... She'll always fear that her babies will someday be born with defects.

I know, it's so risky. So!

"Stop it! STOP IT, DAMN IT, STOPITSTOPITSTOPIT!" I shout at the setting sun, but it couldn't care less. The unrequited love between people and sunsets. Sunsets don't give a shit about our ridiculous problems.

See? She's shouting now because she knows we're telling the truth. It might be too late for her to purge Annie from her body!

I can't fool myself anymore. Car horns, ambulance sirens, a family argument from the upper floors perhaps – all that could float up to the roof. But the flat-toned remarks of this threesome devoted to discussing me? The blood freezes in my veins. The Voices never belonged to people in the bar, or in the room next door. Or on the street. They've always been inside my head.

I can't stand being on the roof any longer. I climb down – still in one piece, despite my erratic state. Sometimes you don't need to be strong or sensible. Just lucky. Instinctively, my feet head for The Mockingbird. I'm not on the schedule for tonight, but I need Bartender. Can't think of anyone else who can give me sound advice without sending me off to a mental hospital. Annie used to play that role, but I haven't had a worthy conversation with her recently. She's been chuckling into her hands madly, creeping me out, every time the Voices start speaking. Not her pleasant *PFRRSS-MHOO-MHOO*. It's something else now. Something spine-chilling.

It's early and it's just Bartender and Antoine. I don't mind her presence. That's the thing about people like Antoine – you're not embarrassed to blurt out even the craziest thoughts in front of them.

I'm trying to explain about the Voices. I haven't slept for a really long time and I'm aware that the words roll off my tongue incoherently, beads from a broken necklace. I can't pull myself together. I grab onto the bar, hold on for dear life, feeling that if I let go I'll fall from the roof. The skin on my fingers is bitten, with the occasional drop of blood.

Nevertheless, Bartender understands me.

"Alice! You need to calm down! It's not the end of the world. Now I want you to go home. Antoine will give you a lift, and then you'll go to bed and have a good, long sleep! Okay?"

"What do you mean, it's not the end of the world?! I've been hearing VOICES! That's… I'm a schizophrenic!"

"Listen, princess, you really do need to calm down!" Antoine chimes in. "A standard amphetamine psychosis – everybody who's overdosed has been there. I've also heard voices; once it was so bad that I kept seeing this shadowy face stalking me in the corner of my peripheral vision. When I turned around, there was no one there. That's how out of it I was. I went to see a doctor and he gave me some pills. *Film-coated tablets*, the pill bottle read. Hilarious! I'm living in a film alright, I thought, and now I've got the film-coated pills to go with it!" Antoine is chuckling hard, obviously very pleased with this story. "You never know what sort of trip a *film-coated* pill might take you on… Anyway, I didn't take them. Aren't we a lovely little bunch? We're firmly against prescribed drugs because doctors are in league with the pharmaceutical mafia in this grand conspiracy to screw our bodies and minds and get us addicted. But street drugs? Give it here, sure, no problem! As long as it's illegal, as long as it's my own rebellious decision, poisoning is quite welcome!" She laughs melodically again, and so do I through my tears. Story of my life too. "Anyway, I'm fine now. When I take it easy with the silly stuff, everything's fine. Sometimes I get carried away and the Voices are back. But I'm the sort of person who adapts to mad voices rather swiftly. I just know that when I stop snorting they'll go away, and I even entertain myself by noting down what they say…"

"Some entertainment!" Bartender bristles. "Enough of this shit, Antoine! Take her home. She goes to bed and she stays clean as of tomorrow. I'll personally keep an eye on you, Alice!"

In the car Antoine keeps trying to stop me from panicking. Amphetamine psychosis only resembles schizophrenia, she says. It's not the real thing.

"You stop using and the hallucinations are gone. Well, unless you've got some hereditary mental disorder lurking in the depths of your mind – drugs can work as a trigger, you know… But don't worry, darling, I don't think that's the case here."

She drops me off in front of my place. I got this, I insist, I'll be fine on my own. As I turn to face the entrance, however, I already hate everyone who left me all alone at this horrible moment. I unlock the door and turn on every possible light so I don't have to listen to the Voices in the dark. Then I realize that the light terrifies me even more. Shaking and whimpering, I turn everything back off, leaving only the bedside lamp on. I try lying down on the bed, but feel fully exposed and vulnerable there, so I grab my teddy bear and cuddle him in a corner of the room. Bury my exhausted body and head under a blanket. Continue talking to myself through the sobs, struggling to drown out the Voices. They're still here. I've always wondered how people in horror movies just fall asleep when they know something's lurking in the dark. Eventually, I fall asleep too. Literally fall. It feels like going down a dark abyss, the dizziness, the tight stomach and everything, and all I can think about is that I might never wake up.

For the next couple of days I'm sleepy all the time. I feel sick and sink into thoughts about how I've ruined my life. However, the Voices grow ever quieter. Eventually they shut up – forever, I hope. In a while my sense of smell returns too, along with the joyful feeling of being alive.

Annie's absence didn't induce the desperate fever I'd expected. Antoine was right. "It's not hard to quit," she'd said back in the car. "Amphetamine abstinence isn't that bad, you won't be chewing on the bed sheets like folks on H do." Still, I want to do her one last time. It just doesn't feel right to part with Annie with the bad memories of hallucinations and an imagined pregnancy between us.

"I wish I could see her the way she used to be during our first months together." I'm at the bar, sipping on a virgin cocktail while talking to Bartender and Antoine. I'm staying away from booze for now because it'll surely get me to call Annie. "She was so energetic. Groovy. Full of exciting ideas. No nasty side effects."

"Jesus, Alice!" Bartender is pissed. Drops a glass he's been washing and it almost breaks. He turns off the water, dries his hands on his jeans. "You're like a little kid who knows a movie by heart but wants to see it like a hundred times, over and over again! Don't you get it already? Annie is fun. Until she isn't. Your movie is no longer fun!"

"But the inspiration she gave me!" I insist. "What if I can't tap into creativity without her?"

"Okay." Bartender waves his hands about kind of aimlessly, not sure how to incorporate them into expressing his thoughts. "Try to see it this way. Creative ideas are like rooms in your mind, right? They're fully furnished, only the lights are off. Drugs don't build or furnish your rooms. Everything's already there. Annie helped you turn the lights on, that's all. And you can learn how to turn a goddamn light on by yourself, Alice!"

"Trust me,
we'll figure it out!"

Beautifully put. However, Antoine winks at me in a way that suggests she has something more exciting to offer. She waits for Bartender to walk away, then pulls something like a business card out of her leather bag. Holds it out between two fingers, her thin eyebrow arching into a meaningful expression.

One side of the card reads:

FILM-COATED PILLS CLUB

On the back there's a map with a pin marking a downtown location.

"What's that?" I ask.

"A club for folks like us, mad about exploring the mind's potential with the aid of stimulants. You just adore how stimulants urge you to muse things over in great detail, right? Still, your own imagination can only go so far. In the Film-Coated Pills club, we channel this grand mental energy towards carefully curated topics that my crowd and I have established to provide a particularly exciting experience for someone who's high. Interested?"

I nod vigorously, like a bobblehead dog on a moving truck.

"We convene every first Friday of the month," Antoine carries on in a down-to-business tone. "Meaning that there's a meeting scheduled for next Friday. You're welcome, but certain prerequisites must be met!"

"Like what?" My mind's irrevocably made up. I'm in.

Well done, Alice!

Well down!

"Right, the most crucial requirement is that you're up for using that day. Otherwise you won't be able to achieve the desired states of mind we're after. The second requirement is that you snap some photos with a real camera. Look through a viewfinder and stuff, you know. You do have a camera, right?"

"Not really," I say. "I have this old compact one, but the lens's cracked. Spots appear on every picture."

"Oh, but that's wonderful! It'll make it even more interesting for you!" Antoine straightens up on her chair with growing excitement. "So, here's the deal. Friday, at lunchtime, you snort a line. Then you go out with your cracked camera and just roam the streets until six. That's when we start. You can snap pictures of whatever catches your fancy. Try to make them the most extraordinary pictures you've ever taken. The point is that as a photographer, you start paying much more attention to everything around you. You see the world with fresh eyes. How many times have you walked around downtown? Still, I bet you've never noticed all the charming balconies, entrance doors, mailboxes and other little gems that will captivate you next Friday. You'll see! And you'll stare into the faces of random strangers with indecent interest. It won't matter if they're perfect or crooked, just if they're intriguing enough for your lens... A thrilling sensation! You won't be able to tear your eyes away from some faces. Stories about them will flood your mind. All of this will help you get into the right mood for the session – more receptive, intense and inspired."

I grin. What she says makes me feel normal. It seems that everyone who hooks up with Annie is invested in bizarre activities. I'm not alone with my catalog of personality types.

"I'll bring Venus too. Is that okay? Your club sounds like something she'd die for. She even likes to shoot on film!"

"No problem, darling, do bring her along. Venus is the perfect little odd fish for our eccentric society. Haha, I remember her once, wringing her hands in panic because some guy was in love with her. He supposedly stalked her around. She also loses her marbles when she snorts! But don't do the photography exercise together! Each of you should undergo your own preparation."

"Got it!"

"One last thing, princess… Don't expect some sort of pleasant catharsis. The point of Film-Coated Pills isn't to make us feel good, it's to get us to explore the darkest corners of the mind. That's what we're after."

Friday, June 1st. Lunchtime. I'm sitting at the kitchen table, a porcelain plate in front of me, and in the plate lies Annie, also porcelain-hued, aching for me to breathe her in. Nausea swept over me when I first opened the Ziploc bag and the smell of burned plastic hit my nose. Seems I've developed a physical repulsion to Annie along with a psychological one. Still, I want to see what's going on at the Film-Coated Pills club and I'll stick to Antoine's instructions. I lean over, become one with her once again, like so many times throughout the past year. A hard snort. The bitter taste hits my throat; it's disgusting. It takes effort not to puke, but then the effect kicks in and man, it's not bad. The long-missed relaxed euphoria spreads across my body with a pleasant shiver. I take the camera off its charger and go out.

Clouds fill the sky. A pitch-perfect afternoon for my mission.

"Enough pictures of the clouds, Alice," Annie says soon. "Turn your camera to the street. Amateur photographers are always obsessed with clouds, but you can't find the essence of things there."

Further on into the afternoon, I experience every piece of magic Antoine was talking about. I discover unexpected treasures in familiar places; treasures I've never noticed before. Now, all of a sudden, I see them and they make great pictures. It feels like I'm in a parallel universe. I come across people who are dressed in a way that would normally strike me as over the top, but today I love it. It brings life to the portraits. Annie makes me see myself as a real photographer who's just discovering her talent. I'm well aware that the sense of glory will vanish as soon as she does, but I go along with the lie, daydreaming about exhibitions. I shoot so much that I have to search for places to recharge the camera battery, and I have to delete most of the pictures in order to free space for new ones.

Then it's five thirty and I'm already at the address on the business card. All I can see are locked garages and a small shop.

ADULT DIAPERS

This can't be it. I walk further down the cobbled street, but then I turn back. This time I notice a minute black sign on the side of the diaper shop. "Film-Coated Pills Club," it whispers. I walk in to find Antoine filling in a cash book behind the counter. Her bearing makes everything else look black and white. It's like seeing a phoenix pecking at a nondescript worm in a make-shift wooden cage. I can picture Antoine selling wigs, coffee, shoes, mobile phone accessories... In fact I can picture her almost anywhere, but if someone had asked me where I definitely wouldn't expect to find her, I'd reply: "In an adult diaper shop or at the fishmongers." So all we need is a few headless mackerel here.

Antoine closes the cash book and waltzes toward me, her body taut as a bowstring. Kisses me on both cheeks.

"Welcome, dear!"

"What on earth is this?!"

"Ah!" she waves dismissively. "Don't mind the nappies. Grandpa Marin – who happens to be my grandpa – struck lucky with restitution. When I asked him if I could use the place, he told me that he was planning to open a shop for nappies and other goods for the elderly. The thing is, he's got a house in the suburbs and he runs a care home there. That's how he got it into his mind that he needed a shop too. I just wanted to be able to use the back room for the meetings, didn't care about the front. So I told him I'd manage the shop for him."

Other club members start to show up, mostly women and gay men. Eventually it's a crowd of about fifteen crammed into spaces between diaper packages and boxes of blood pressure monitors. Antoine introduces me to every newcomer. Explains that she's adamant – if you want to be part of Film-Coated Pills, you must be using either coke or some form of amphetamine. The only exception is for an older girl who is on weight loss pills, but according to Antoine, most weight loss pills are essentially amphetamines.

Venus is running late. We wait for her, and when she arrives we all enter the back room. It's bigger than I expected. Big enough to accommodate the necessary number of yoga mats already spread on the floor. A bit too many for the space available, but at least each one has a cushion on it. There are candles too, and music playing. What, is that an Edith Piaf drill remix? All you need to feel dizzy.

Antoine – our mentor – gives a short introductory speech, distributes blindfolds and directs us to lie down on the mats. Specifically reminds the first-timers that the photography task was the fun part; now it's time for deep shit.

"The séance we're about to immerse ourselves in isn't a form of health therapy or liberating meditation. Our aim is to delve into some of the darkest corners of our consciousness and share our experiences simply because we find it fascinating to do so. It's not unlikely that we will return even more disturbed than before. Today's theme is 'Fear.' If anything, tonight you'll get to speak about personal things that you haven't yet had the courage to share with anyone."

Antoine is both the cobra and the snake charmer. She tells you to do something and you don't even consider arguing. Next thing I know, we're all lying on the floor, eyes blindfolded, reaching into the murky water of our memories. Dragging out our deepest fears by the hair. I honestly don't think I get the point of all this, but it's overwhelmingly eerie – the airless room, the dusk, the trembling voices of the other members mixed up with the music. Venus is lying next to me and we hold hands. We squeeze hands.

Her turn comes first.

She begins with some standard fears from early childhood. Gives a brief description of her relationship with her mother. The same story I've already heard – that everyone used to tsk-tsk about how a sociable, vivid persona like the Russian prima donna could have such a pent-up daughter.

"There was only one person who found me more interesting than my mother. My stepfather."

This last bit is a surprise. I squeeze her hand even tighter as I listen to the bitter confession. Her mother's second husband had the perverse habit of opening the bathroom door while Venus was showering, his eyes groping her still-immature curves from a distance. He hinted that "this would be all" as long as she didn't show defiance and lock the door. So she didn't. He never actually tried anything else, but every night when he was home, Venus lay in bed with the light off, not making a sound to avoid drawing his attention.

"Did you tell your mother?" Antoine interrupts our stories every now and then.

"I didn't know how. But I did tell my grandma."

Her grandmother was furious. Spoke about the sexual harassment both with Venus's mother and her real father. No one did anything. The Russian refused to believe it, and Venus's father simply muttered a few hollow threats.

"Every child trusts that Mom and Dad will be there to protect them from freaks. And when you're proven wrong, you start fearing everything. What hurt the most was that my mother divorced him over something else. She couldn't swallow the fact that he cheated on her with another actress. That was reason enough for her to divorce him. Him harassing me wasn't."

No wonder Venus is so needy for love. I just can't fathom where her astounding trust in people comes from.

Soon it's my turn to confide.

My first conscious memory of being terrified goes back to my first year of day care. I'm sitting on a potty in a tiled room with other potties around. I see Mom pass by the door on her way out of the center, and I start to cry. She turns to

208

me; she's crying too. Leaves me there nonetheless. I guess she had to. I go on, screaming with tears. The teacher comes in and slaps me twice. I guess she also had to. Then I'm in the big room. All the kids are sitting in a circle on the carpet. The teacher's telling them some fearsome stories about a Boogeyman who ate children, and I have to sit in the corner as punishment for my misbehavior on the potty. Aloof from the herd, I'd make the easiest victim for the Boogeyman. Thunder cracks outside.

"Nice one," I hear Antoine's voice as if from afar. "Keep going deeper!"

My father drinks. As could be expected, this influences certain aspects of my childhood in predictable ways. Similar to what Venus described, I'd persuade my mom to go to bed early and turn the lights off, so that he wouldn't pick a fight with her when (and if) he got home. I honestly believe that all parents – even if they suck at parenting – love their children. But you need much more than love to keep your child from repeatedly falling asleep on a tear-stained pillow.

Dad never hit my sister or me. He was never rude to us; we were his babies. I was always worried about my mom though. I feared that something awful might happen, worse than that time he pushed her down the stairs while she was pregnant and I thought I might not get to have a sister. But growing up in a home filled with scandals did have a bright side: I was hardly ever intimidated by bullies at school. You think yelling and threats will scare me? You think getting punched in the face will ruin my day? Come to my house and see for yourself, Bully! You'll have to do a lot better than that.

Next memory. The little park where we used to play as kids was near the construction site of the Museum of Military

History (they never completed the building and the museum is now located elsewhere). It was a large construction site with a huge pit, its sandy walls loose and dangerous, surrounded by tanks, combat aircrafts and statues of lions. What kid wouldn't jump the fence to play there?

Once a boy from school shut me in one of the tanks. I've never been claustrophobic so I wasn't scared at first. Just sat there waiting to be released. Then I saw the dead frog. Being stuck in a narrow space – fine. Being stuck with a carcass – scream, scream, SCREEEAM! I might've woken the frog from its eternal sleep. I couldn't calm down long after they took me out of the tank and I started to have nightmares of people pouring bags of toads over me. I know that frogs are basically harmless, but I've been terrified of them ever since.

After my experience in the tank, death became a *thing*. It had a smell and a sound associated with it. Smelled like a rusty swamp; sounded like silence, faintly interrupted by the distant construction-site noise of the neighborhood.

As kids we had another macabre attraction, one that still gives me the creeps. The morgue of the Medical University was located just across from my primary school. In fact, it's still there and if you happen to pass by, you'll surely sense the stench of rotting flesh wafting along the boulevard. The windows at the sidewalk level are covered with thick blinds but if you stand really close, if you lean on the window and peek through the ventilator opening, you'll get to see a hall of old autopsy tables, channels for the blood carved into them. The first time I mustered the courage to stand close and lean in, all I saw was a sheet with unsettling rusty red stains on one of the tables. It wasn't enough to put me off. The second time there were bodies in terrifying positions, one of them cut open. The new pair of gloves I was wearing absorbed the smell of the morgue. Back home I scrubbed them relentlessly with soap, but no matter what I did, they still reeked. New nightmares followed – for months I'd wake up in the middle of the night, my face drenched in tears.

Nothing, however, compares to my new acquisition: fear of the Voices. Before that, my greatest fear used to be death. It didn't feel wrong to fear death. Dying is horrifying – no big deal, pretty normal. It can even be seen as a good thing since it means you appreciate life. The Voices though … they make me realize that while I'm still here, and living, something terrible could happen inside my own head; so terrible that it might make me wish I were dead. Still, despite myself, despite the all-consuming fear, I'm here with Annie again. I'm a person who has seen addiction and abuse, yet I still go ahead and get hooked up and allow myself to lose it and hit people too.

Now I'm scared of myself.

The grim memory-digging comes to an end. We all get up, but our eyes remain nailed to the floor. Everyone's silent. Antoine asks for another two minutes of our time to explain what the next séance will be about.

"Sexual fantasies. It's open only for people whose partners are also into taking uppers. Naturally, your partners are welcome too! I'll show you a selection of film excerpts. Yes, you guessed correctly, it's porn I'm talking about. Not just any porn though. These will be films with unnerving plots that can arouse just about anyone, although few would care to admit it. Your assignment will be to act out the scenes with your partner after you leave. Point is that under normal circumstances you'd never admit to wanting such play, perhaps not even to yourself. Now, however, you will have an excuse. I made you do it. And I don't mean fantasies that feel more or less acceptable: bondage, soft SM, group sex. It's fairly easy to admit to such things. But what about taboo thoughts like incest or bestiality, or Lolita-style stories? Personally, even I find them repulsive when done in real life. But after I saw those films, the images kept popping up in my head when I had sex, and they drove me wild with desire. Do you have the nerve to go to such lengths? The only risk is that afterward, sex without drugs and such fantasies might never seem satisfying enough… And one more thing: you might want to book a room somewhere for this… Not everyone would dare to do such things at home!"

I'm certainly skipping this one. Someday – maybe. But right now the last thing I need is to mess with my potential sexual deviance.

Enough of exploring ways to lose my mind.

I'm putting an end to my life with Annie. This time for real. Otherwise, what's the difference between me and glue-huffing Ronaldo? I leaf through the pages I've written over the last few months and it seems like things really did happen around me before. Now things happen mostly within the confines of my head. Psychology lessons my ass! It's not a brunch crowd I've been dealing with. It's people who've been drinking and using and whatnot – of course they're all messed up. Working in a bar, becoming best friends with a high-school student, doing drugs. All actions of someone who's trying to dodge the responsibility of taking life seriously. Squiggle pills for girls older than Pippi Longstocking, forever searching for the medication that will make us never grow up.

I can't force myself to be serious in life. It's not something you force yourself into, it's a process. And I don't feel ready to settle down yet. I need to experience more troubled worlds before I learn to value peace. But it's important to balance mental exploration with physical exploration, otherwise there's a risk of losing your mind. That's why I need to go away, so for now my exams and my book will have to wait. It's time for me to explore a new country the same way I explored Signland. I've decided to find a job in a circus somewhere in Europe. Why not actually live out the experience that has proven so alluring to mythomaniacs? There must be someone who will take me on; I'm even ready to work without payment. Hard physical labor will do me good.

First, however, I need to say goodbye to Venus and Tino. We made plans to go to the coast for a few days and I still intend to follow through with them. I need to figure things out with Bartender too. I have some feelings to confess there…

But most importantly, I have to break up with my Annie forever.

Quit seeing her, period.

Period.

.

I hope.

Excerpts from Alice's Dream Journal #2

April 25th

I dreamed I had an appointment at the main entrance of the zoo. I can't remember who I was supposed to meet, but in my dream I knew; I also knew we were on a special mission of sorts. As I slept on, I got the feeling that I remembered these details from an earlier dream. I've experienced this before: the certainty that I'm watching a "sequel" to an earlier dream. I waited and waited but no one showed up. The entrance of the zoo looked more like a shopping mall entrance, but on the other side of the fence it was the same as the zoo in reality. I walked in. I was to accomplish the mission alone. I don't remember what it was; I think I was searching for something. I saw all the cages and the enclosures, and they appeared just as I remembered them in real life: the concrete lower world of the bears, the stinky building with the big cats, the overgrown grass between the tiles in front of the bird cages... Only in this zoo, there wasn't a single animal. I passed by people, and they all stared at me as if I were the beast on display. I couldn't accomplish the mission, whatever

it was, and eventually I remembered that in fact the appointment was for the following day. Then all of a sudden it was
already tomorrow. I was waiting at the entrance again, and the
dream unraveled from the beginning.

As per one dream book, a zoo is supposed to mean "dangerous thoughts that can be harmful to your work." Another
book says it's "journeys to far-away lands, new knowledge
and colorful experiences." This second interpretation suits me
fine.

May 14th

I dreamed that I gave birth to a child. A baby girl. Giving
birth itself was nothing special, it just happened. What I remember most clearly from the dream took place afterward.
As I was pushing the newborn's pram, the baby suddenly sat
up and started talking to me fluently, like an older child. I
don't remember what she said, but it can't mean anything
good.

"If you are a baby or a baby speaks to you, you will witness some fraud, some deceit."

May 21st

In my dream Venus was dying my hair. Blue. I had a date
and I was super happy with my new, sexy, blue-haired look.

Dream book: "If you dye your hair yourself, then you
are lying to yourself and to other people. If someone else
dyes your hair for you – be cautious, a close person is lying
to you!"

Well, with Tino in our lives, no surprise there.
Wait! Do I believe in dreams now?

June 8th

I dreamed that all my teeth fell out. First only one of them was loose on one side. A piece broke off, then the whole tooth came out and fell to the ground. Two more teeth were loose now. I went to the dentist immediately. His office was in the middle of a field, but still it had a white door with a number on it. As I waited in front of the door, both of the loose teeth broke apart in my mouth. It felt as if I was chewing on sand. I started crying uncontrollably, as I was already certain I'd wind up with no teeth at all. I have no idea how I'd react to this in real life, but in my dream it felt like the worst tragedy ever. When the dentist finally called me in, there was almost nothing left in my mouth. However, he reassured me that in an hour or two new teeth would come through.

I went back home, losing a couple of wisdom teeth on the way there. I stood in front of the bathroom mirror. My mouth was black. My last two teeth fell out into the sink and they were black too. I went back to crying. I realized that no matter what the dentist told me, I'd never have teeth again.

I woke up still crying, the metallic taste of blood in my mouth. I looked at the screen of my phone — 06:06.

I made the mistake of looking all this up in the dream book and consulting a few websites too. They were all explicit: "If you lose a tooth in your dream, someone will die. If it's a molar or a wisdom tooth, a distant acquaintance will pass away, but if it's a front tooth, it will be a close relative."

I made the even bigger mistake of reading the users' comments. They all said that after they dreamed about their teeth falling out, people close to them actually did die. What about me? I'd lost all my teeth in one dream; does this mean that over thirty people in my family and friends will die soon? Or should I prepare for my own death? This is total nonsense!

Olly Olly Oxen Free

I always count when I travel. I don't know why, it's just a thing I've done since I was a kid, you know. On the bus, I usually count the windows of the swanky buildings along the way. In the car, I count the red vehicles we pass by. Or the blue ones. Or whatever. On the train, I usually count the electric poles in the fields.

So this happens a few summers ago, all right? We're on the train, on our way to the coast. I sit by the window, counting the poles flash by. They flash by like ghosts. I got a bad feeling, the kind of antsy anxiety dude gets when something fucked up's coming. I figure the fucked up thing's gonna happen to me. At the time, it doesn't cross my mind that it's meant for my buddies, Venus and Alice. A fine pair of girls they are, beautiful and smart babes, but still dopeheads, all right? It's a damn shame. I mean, most of the dope head girls I know are just as shit beautiful and smart. I don't know why that is.

So, we're on our way to this trendy campsite by the sea. Some friends of Venus's mom keep their classy new caravan there for the whole summer. Cool crib. They invite friends to use it when they're away, what with them paying for the place anyway, and all. Point is, we're gonna crash in a caravan. If it hadn't been a caravan, if it was just a regular guest house or whatever, with a regular toilet, then probably none of this shit would've happened.

We plan to stay there for four days tops, still these two show up at the train station dragging along two suitcases about yay big. Huge. With floral patterns. What's in there, I ask, and they giggle. Clothes, hehe. So they got this huge amount of clothes for four days, all right, but they don't take half of the stuff they really need. Like a bikini or toothpaste, you know. So that's Venus and Alice for you – heads in the clouds, super impractical. But that's kinda their charm too, you know, I'll give them that. They chatter excitedly, leaving me in charge of the suitcases. They're totally amped to stay clean from now on, starting with the vacation.

I start drinking as soon as we get on the train. All of a sudden they both fall asleep, then I'm counting poles on my own. Venus's head in my lap feels heavy, makes me think about our relationship. I don't know what my problem is. I'm not even sure I wanna be with her anymore. I appreciate her sweetness and all, you know what I mean, I like her a lot, we have a real cool time together. Okay, maybe sex with her isn't exactly off the charts, I wanna say, she ain't much into kinky stuff and all that. But she's all, like, crazy about me, so I don't care that much about sex. At the same time I wanna be with Alice too. She's hot, you know. I got a feeling that about half the ladies I'll see at the coast will seem hot to me too… And I swear to God, I really wanna believe in beautiful love without cheating and all that! I don't know, guess that's why I tell all the girls the story about the penguins, and the story about my pops too. He painted the first graffiti in town for my mom! Totally freaky! I respect that, but my own love life's pretty wild. The one long-term relationship I had? We totally busted it! In the beginning she was right on to do all kinds of crazy stuff for me, you know. I liked that. We had a good thing going before we moved in together. Next thing I know, passion starts cooling down as soon as your girl starts feeling comfortable taking a dump in front of you… She starts neglecting herself, putting on weight and all… You know how it is. All of a sudden she's fricking boring. I can't even remember what the interesting stuff we talked about for the first couple months was. *I miss you*, she texts me after I hit the road. And I'm like, *I've missed you for a year and a half, bitch.* I never went back to her. Now on the train I debate whether or not to do something like that to Venus too.

The big blue aspirin. Grandpops used to say that the sea could cure anything. Guess he didn't mean drug addiction.

After we get off the train, we've gotta hitchhike to the campsite. So this dude picks us up. He's super twitchy, you know, got all kinds of tics, constantly tugs at something, adjusts things, rubs his nose, makes funny sounds with his throat… We stop at a gas station, and before he gets out of the car he touches the plastic logo on the steering wheel to make sure it's fixed in place. He obviously removes it regularly. I know what this means.

"Girls, this bitch is a dealer! You feel like jacking a dealer?"

Venus and Alice, they cream for such dumb-ass ideas. So I'm on. They cheer from the backseat as I reach for the steering wheel and remove the cover, super careful with my moves. I grab the Ziploc bag that's jammed into the hollow space. Not some small Ziploc bag. No. Massive bag, about yay big. So I stuff it in my pants, all right? Next, dude comes back and we tell him we changed our minds, we wanna go to another campsite now, further south. This way he won't be able to locate us when he finds out the stash's missing. Plan works all right. He drops us off further south, we say our sweet goodbyes, then walk back to our campsite.

The guy's stuff is killer. Best shiz we ever laid our noses on. So much for the girls' intentions to stay off. They dip in the sea just once, rest of the time they rock 24/7, snorting like crazy. As for me, I keep drinking too. I'm lost and I don't feel like coming down. I drink from sunrise to sunrise. I mean, literally. I don't give a shit I'm at the coast. Grandpops taught me to love the sea, swim, play in the waves and all, but now I don't do jack shit other than, you know, keep drinking. I'm doing the same thing I do everywhere. I'm drinking, okay? One day pretty much blends into the next, only there's more gulls than pigeons around here.

I've been thinking a lot about what happened. If I could turn the clock back, I'd ditch drinking. I'd do Venus right, love her with all my heart and whatever. I'd do anything and everything to, like, save her and Alice from the crap. I'd totally… But that's not how it happened. I didn't do shit. I was too busy drinking and partaking in their snorting.

…Four… Five… Six…

By the end of day one I quit keeping track of the lines we blow. We buy enough smokes and booze for the entire stay, scarcely any food, and then there's no cash left. And by no cash I mean nada, zip, zilch, to the extent that we ain't got nothing to roll a tube from. For snorting, you know. I usually like to use a straw for snorting, but no straws lying around either.

"We seriously ain't got a single bill in this joint?!"

"We do, actually."

Alice points at the Monopoly box. They brought it along in the flower-patterned suitcases, you know, *in case we felt like playing.*

So we play. We roll a Monopoly bill into a tube. And we snort. It's like a sick patchwork of childhood and junkiedom. Wasted as I am, the bad feeling from the train still throbs in my mind. I wave it off, figuring it must come from that weird, trippy, dizzy sensation you get when you're spending your first nights by the sea. You know what I mean?

On the afternoon of the third day, I puke by a tree. My vomit's green because today I'm drinking cocktails with mint liqueur.

...Seven... Eight... Nine...

I remember this one time when I was a kid and we played hide-and-seek in the neighborhood park. I saw some wasted older kid puking in the bushes and I laughed at him. Venus and Alice must have rubbed this off on me, you know – every time they're high they start remembering lame-ass stuff from their childhood.

I notice a couple little girls on a bench nearby. Once I'm done puking, I go over to bother them some.

"Olly olly oxen free!" I say.

The kids look at a loss.

"What, you don't know what 'olly olly oxen free' means?"

"Nope. You tell us!"

"It's a hide-and-seek thing. The one who's it can't find you and they shout 'olly olly oxen free' and start counting to ten, giving you a chance to leave your hiding place and get to home base before they finish counting –"

"We don't play hide-and-seek," they say. "We don't want our clothes to get all dirty."

Little brats! I leave them be and go back to the caravan. And there I find Alice, and she's all messed up. She's never reeked of sweat before, you know, and now she stinks, her eyes fixed on a point in front of her. There's something in her eyes, man, something dead.

My memory of what happens next is hazy. In hindsight, I realize we totally overreacted and our reactions were misguided. We were stoned. Imagined things that weren't there. But I don't know that at the time, okay? The shit makes me kinda paranoid, I mean, Jesus, anyone would be pretty frigging paranoid after three days of snorting. And Venus? She's fucking nuts with paranoia.

It all starts with her. She bounces into the caravan and starts looking around slam-bang. That's how people look around when they're high on dope – *slam-bang*. I ain't got no idea what she's looking around for, but regardless of my own state of delirium I notice that she's moving her head way too much, way more than is needed for looking around. Her face's twisted and twitching with fear.

"I'm being followed! This guy followed me all the way here from the bathrooms! The entire way! Now he's out front, and he's got a gun!"

I ignore her convulsive protests and push the little curtain aside to take a look. Dude looks back at me – there really is a dude, a cue-ball son of a bitch, eyeballing the caravan hard, and he really does have a gun on his hip. When he catches me peeking at him, dude ducks out of sight. The three of us instantly figure that the cops tracked us down. They're gonna search the place, and with what we got left on us, they're gonna presume we're pushing. It's not a teener, you know, we got like a half or something in here. We must get rid of the stash. Immediately. But how? It's not like we can just flush it down the toilet. We're in a fucking caravan, remember, and fucking caravans ain't got proper toilets where you can just flush stuff down. I freak out. Yeah, I'm scared shitless, all right? My ass is on the line. If they come in and bust us, I'll be in deep shit, 'cause I've had a run-in with the cops already.

So I come up with this damn stupid plan. My teeth rattling nervously, I give each of the girls a role.

"So listen up," I say. "Here's what we gonna do. Venus, you're gonna go outside and find out if dude is gone. If dude is gone, come back quickly and we'll all go and ditch the stuff outside. Now Alice! As soon as Venus is off, we gonna start counting real slow. If she's not back by the count of ten, you and I gonna swallow the lot."

I've heard about dealers doing this to avoid getting caught. Seems like a damn good epic plan at the moment. My hands shaking erratically, I wrap the stuff in pieces of napkin. We gonna swallow them like pills and then the napkin's gonna disintegrate in our stomachs, causing the drug to kick in more slowly.

Alice says yes.

Venus leaves. We start counting, real slow. No sign of Venus.

... Ten!

Still no sign of Venus. Alice and I lock eyes before we go ahead with the plan. I try to remember what I saw in her eyes back then. Was there fear under her lashes? I guess not. She wouldn't expect anything final to come out of this. Uh-uh. Not Alice. She never expected bad things to happen.

We swallow our hand-made pills. A moment later Venus comes back. With her twitchy mouth explains that when she got outside, dude started hitting on her. Apparently he was no cop, just saw her at the bathrooms and liked her, so he followed her to the caravan. She couldn't shake him off before we reached ten, that's why she was late.

As Venus struggles to put an intelligible story together, I start feeling damn sick. Think I'm gonna die. Alice is much worse though. She's spastic. Starts puking. Goes delirious.

Mom... Mom... Don't cry, please, Mom... I didn't mean to...

She's barely making sense now. I'm not sure what she says just before she blacks out but it's something like:

The repeating numbers... Now I'll go and find out...

Venus is crying hysterically, way too zonked to do anything helpful. I can jump ship right now, but I don't do that. I try to call 911 but I'm so screwed I can't unlock my phone for a while. But I can see the clock. Keeps popping up. 16:16. I swear to God, cross my heart, I really got repeating numbers there! May I be struck by lightning if I'm lying! It still creeps me out!

I call an ambulance at last. They arrive and they say Alice is gone.

Oh my god, Alice's voice calling out to her mother… It's still in my ears. Ripped my heart out. Her apologies for dying, you know. All she could think about before going was ruining the life of the woman who'd brought her to life. I've heard that before people die, they often see their deceased old folks in the room with them… That's weird. Our whole life we just go ahead and hurt our parents, abuse their unconditional love, and all we ever care about are some other people, insignificant jerks. Until the day we're on our deathbed. We realize for the first time that nobody has ever been more important to us than our mother. True that. Life has this tricky way of making us figure out what's important in the end. Man's gotta respect his parents more.

God! I wanted to say all this to Alice's mother but I couldn't get my nut up to even speak to her at the funeral. I felt so dickish, all right? She looked at me just once. God! Like she laid that on me, like I was the murderer of her little girl. She'd hit me in the face for hours if she got the chance. But poor woman, she was so torn up she didn't even have the strength to tell me to leave.

Venus didn't come to the funeral. Her mom didn't let her. Word got out that she spent some time in a psychiatric clinic. Last I heard she joined some cult after that. That's all I know.

OUTRO
A life of questions and death?

I found this in Alice's waitress notes. I like it and I think it's an appropriate beginning to the end of her book.

Maybe I should introduce myself first. And apologize – I'm no writer. I'll try to follow Alice's style in my short notes here. Don't be too hard on me if I fail.

I'm Bartender. I don't think I need to go into further detail because Alice already did that.

However, she didn't finish her book.

"I'm not sure where life will take me when I come back from the coast," she told me when she showed up for her last shift at The Mockingbird. She'd announced her decision to quit just a few days earlier, and she was leaving for the coast soon with Venus and Tino. I hadn't had enough time to get used to the idea that her radiant smile wouldn't be there to warm the place up anymore.

"Let's go abroad together! We're bound to try to be together sooner or later!" she said.

We'd never talked about our feelings before, but it didn't come as a surprise. It was obvious that she had something for me.

"It won't work out, kiddo. We don't have a single thing in common. At least at this point."

"Neither of us has social media accounts?" she smiled.

"Yeah. My reasons for that are totally different from yours though."

I spilled out a whole slew of arguments to justify why a hypothetical relationship between us would be a total failure. Now I'm so sorry I did that. I didn't even manage to convince myself.

"But you have to promise me that you won't give up on your book!" I said with more certainty.

"Well, it looks like that's exactly what's gonna happen… My inspiration stuck around for quite a while and I've got most of the chapters completed, but then it dried up. Now I can't think of a good enough ending. Seriously! Nothing worthy comes to mind! It really pisses me off. And what's worse, when I read back over what I wrote a few months ago, it all seems so stupid and naive. I can't see any point in finishing such a lousy job!"

"Stop being a perfectionist, or you'll never accept that your book is completed. That'd be a pity."

"Yeah, right? Screwing up my own dream!"

"Want some help with the ending?"

My father is a publisher so I know a thing or two about books. He told me how most authors are – you always have to push them, otherwise they never consider their work ready for publication. There's always something wrong with their inspiration, they want everything to be perfect, but it never seems perfect of course, so they deny themselves the satisfaction of a job well done.

"If you really don't intend to finish the book, you'd better let someone else write the ending for you. At least your work will get through to the readers instead of collecting dust in your desk drawer."

Alice hesitated at my suggestion. Said she wanted to give her spoiled inspiration more time. So we made a deal: the following day I'd drop by her place and she'd give me the draft. I was granted permission to read it, but she explicitly asked me not to tell her what I thought about it. She said we needed to wait five years – she'd heard somewhere that was how long it took to write a novel. If she hadn't completed and published the book by that time, she'd happily let me help her. It was up to her anyway, but still I felt compelled to express my opinion. "Two years tops." We bargained for a while, as if we were at a flea market, and eventually shook on four years.

The following day I went to her apartment. Declined her invitation to come in and waited at the doorstep. I was afraid that if I went inside, my life would change dramatically. Alice handed me a memory stick with the completed chapters of her book and a rusty chocolate tin full of loose waitress notes. She'd written with a tremulous hand, impossible abbreviations and all. Deciphering all that was hard, and the fact that many of the notes were stained by God knows what didn't help much either. I asked her if she wouldn't need the notes in her attempt to complete the book by herself. Turned out my hunch about the desk drawer was right.

"I type a chapter down on my laptop only after I'm finished with it. Before that I write the drafts by hand. I have three different endings buried in my drawer, so I've already used what I liked from the waitress notes. We'll see if one of these versions makes it to the final draft, or maybe you'll come up with something better that…"

I gave her a hug before I left, maybe a beat too long. As I waited for the elevator, I made a conscious effort not to turn around and wave one last goodbye. I didn't want her to see my tears.

A few days later, just before they set off for the coast, I received this:

Approximately one year ago I told you the story of how I fell in love with Tino. This issue of the Bill will be dedicated to love as well. But this time it's not about me; my dear friend Alice asked to use the platform so she could write a love letter to her Bartender. So here she goes…

You told me you aren't capable of love. But you know, we women have this wondrous talent — the instant we hear something like that, our instinctive reaction is: "So you say you can't love? How interesting! My mission in life will be to change that!" I guess a simple "Stay away from him" would be much wiser, but I'm not giving up on you all the same.

You also told me that you couldn't lose yourself in a girl like me, who's been with so many guys. That you wouldn't trust me if I didn't share every last detail of my past, and then you wouldn't trust me because all the details would have you thinking that a single long-term relationship couldn't satisfy me. Anyway, let's give sharing a try. Let me tell you everything, and then maybe, just maybe, you'll figure out that the exact number of my past affairs could nail me right to your side.

Granted, I scattered my feelings in too many directions. But you see, I'm the species that needs to experience as many worlds as possible before losing interest in diversity. And every Great Love is a separate world, as is

236

every little crush for that matter. The stories that happened to me are trivial. I guess everyone's been there and anyone could've told me in advance how things would unfold, so I needn't have bothered getting hurt.

But I needed to see the end of a dozen worlds so I wouldn't be afraid of an apocalypse anymore.

There's the world where I excitedly got on a plane. A few happy days later, I was back on the plane, crying silently in my seat on the way home.

The world where I was trying to figure out how to break up with my boyfriend. "He'll suffer so much!" Then he went ahead and called an end to it. He didn't suffer that much. So all of a sudden my ego went mental, stuck in the fixation that I couldn't live without that one particular love. It made me beg and whine, say "I want to die!," shed crocodile tears.

The world where a guy went ballistic because I didn't reciprocate his feelings. I only liked him as a friend. He found this a good reason to call me a whore.

The world where my partner and I came up with names for our future children. Remembering that I've shared bedsheets with him is enough to make me puke now.

The world where I was upset with another partner because he never bought me flowers. And the world where I found out how irritating it was to receive flowers on every date.

The world where morning after morning I snoozed my alarm five times just to lie "a bit longer" next to someone. Or the world where another someone motivated me to get up early, to show him how disciplined and energetic I was.

The world where I got together with a guy not because I loved him, but because it seemed I'd never do better than him. I had second thoughts repeatedly, left him a couple of times, then called him again. He was always there. He didn't deserve any of that.

The world where I showed a man my darkest side and he still wanted me.

And a worse world where a man wanted me exclusively because of my dark side. He wasn't mature enough to love me when I grew brighter.

The world where I went to sleep, blissfully certain that I'd wake up next to my new lover. I woke up next to his goodbye letter.

The world where a guy told me that he wanted us to split up because of fifteen things about me that he found really annoying and couldn't change or tolerate. The moment I found another world (with another man), my ex suddenly forgot all about his list of fifteen things and wanted badly to get back together with me.

The world where I "accidentally" left my stuff at his place. I needed an excuse to return.

The world where a man did everything to get me, almost forced me to fall in love with him, only to push me away without explanation a couple of days later.

The world where I experienced financial love–sickness. Happens every time you break up with someone who earns much more than you. You get used to his standards. And after it's gone, your depression is worse than ever because you have to go back to sneaking peeks at taximeters and considering restaurant menu prices. As despicable as it sounds, let's face it – it's easier to recover from love when you have enough money.

The world where I still loved a guy who'd dumped me. And that feeling pushed me into an angry, emotionless episode of fleeting affairs with different men.

The world where I checked my phone every three min-utes. I was itching to do it even more often, but I tried to occupy myself with other things in between.

The world where a guy called me about a hundred times a day, for some reason convinced that it wouldn't annoy me. Or the world where another guy would promise to call me in the evening, and then he'd reappear days later with a cheerful tone as if nothing had happened.

The world of the attic studio. Passionate raindrops rolling down the small window. We could spend three days in a row there without going out, naked and wet, the scent of sex lingering everywhere. One day I climbed into his jeans to go to the supermarket for frankfurters and bread. On the street I realized there was nothing in our relationship but sex. I never went back to the studio. The jeans are still in my closet.

There was another world with exceptional amounts of sex too, in an exceptional number of locations. We even made a list of the places.

Throughout my experience of the early worlds of love, I was at a loss. I had no idea how to express any of my feelings. And they were so pure! After an overabundance of encounters and farewells, I grew colder inside, but cold or not, I learned to show my love perfectly well, although it no longer feels as pure and true as it used to. I make the best chicken soup when someone catches a cold. I'm trained to utter and provoke I love you's, but they all seem kind of automated now… Even the pain afterwards seems automated. The most heartbreaking moment was when I finally realized that the easiest way to hold someone's interest was to leave after sex. No sleepovers. Isn't that sad!

We're one-winged, one-armed creatures. Forever striving for perfection, never able to reach anything close to it. No other species strives for perfection. No other species is so doomed not to achieve it. The truth is, we humans have this inherent love for drama, and it's so hard for us to stop falling for problematic people. Romeo and Juliet had it easy. Back then, all you had to do was love someone your family didn't approve of, and the drive for self-destruction would be thus satisfied. Now? We choose all kinds of freaks to serve our bad instincts. Maybe that's the whole problem of our modern society – we have so much choice in everything that we feel more lost than ever. Too responsible for our actions. We are free to choose our profession. The country we live in. We are free to choose our diet. Our sex. We are even free to choose our god. How overwhelming is that?

Anyway, I can only regret the things I haven't done. I don't have any regrets about the experiences I've had because of love, but I'm bored now. The once-excitingly complicated worlds have become repetitive and I no longer find any thrill in suffering. I've grown tired of men who make me unhappy. Good guys seem much more mysterious to me now.

I'll be thrilled by a relationship where I get to feel nice. With the Perfect Guy — the one who instills respect without hurting me, who makes me change without demanding change, who is perfect because he's got all my favorite imperfections. And I think this guy might be you. When you held me in your arms on my doorstep, I felt that you were nothing like a Siberian Husky. Huskies are beautiful, they like you, wag their tail at you, but a few moments later they wag it at the girl next door too. And if you try to take their freedom away, you'll come across as the worst person ever. But you, you're a St. Bernard. Comfortable, gentle, composed. You make me feel protected.

I'll come back for you!

P.S. Do you know the most beautiful expression of hope I've ever seen? It's from The Little Prince.

Just two curving lines and a little star above them. Exupéry asks you to remember this "landscape." He is convinced that if you see it in person you'll recognize it. And perhaps you'll let him know that the Little Prince has come back. It's not only beautiful, it's also the most accurate expression of hope. Just two curving lines and a star.

I hope we'll meet again someday, Bartender.

Almost four years have passed since Alice wrote that. She's still in my thoughts. If one day our paths do cross again, I'll try to be with her. I hope she'll be wise enough not to hurt me. In the meantime, I did some thorough research – no book by the title of *Alice on a Friday Night* has been published. It's time for me to attend to that dream then.

I guess you expect me to clarify the matter of Alice's death. The truth is, I don't know the truth.

We haven't heard of Alice or her friends since she left The Mockingbird. She'd become close with some of the regulars and they missed her but couldn't get in touch. When I last saw her, she warned me that she was going to get a new phone number. She believed everyone should once in a while purge the people they socialized with; only immediate friends got your new number, and if someone else was really important, life would certainly find a way to bring you back together. I liked this philosophy. When I left the bar later that same year, I changed my number too.

After a while, life caused me to cross paths with Tino again. I met a guy at a bar, and in the course of our conversation he mentioned where he lived; it was pretty close to that punk's apartment building. So I asked my new acquaintance if he knew Tino.

"Tino? Seriously?! Haha, you know what we call him in the neighborhood? Truthful Tino. That dude would lie to his own mother about the name she gave him!"

The guy told me stuff that only confirmed most of the things I'd already suspected. Alice has given you an extensive idea about the List of Lies. I'll just add that Tino's never attended any film academy (although he's cut out for it really), and he's never worked at the airport.

"I knew he was bullshitting us about everything! Fucking nutjob! Not that I give a shit about him, but he had two girls I knew trapped in his lies."

"You don't by any chance mean the girls he took to the coast?" My informer's face suddenly dropped. "That sucked, man…"

"What do you mean?"

That's how I learned about Alice's alleged overdose. That summer Tino came back from the coast with the story of Alice dying and Venus going insane. No one in the neighborhood knew them well enough to have any contacts and verify Tino's narrative.

As I listened to the whole tragedy, I held tight to my conviction that it couldn't be true. Just another example of the damn bastard's bullshit! Still, my heart missed a beat every time I thought there was a tiny chance that Tino hadn't lied this time. Sometimes the most terrifying stories turn out to be true. But Alice hates gossip. She hates it when people judge others on a word-of-mouth basis. I couldn't mourn her solely based on hearsay, could I? So I went to her place, only to find out her family had moved. Since they hadn't lived there for very long, I couldn't find any neighbors who knew them well enough to provide me with helpful information.

After some effort I managed to locate Tino. I told him that I'd heard about Alice's death. I too played a role; pretended that I didn't hate him, that it never crossed my mind his disgusting story might be a lie. I persuaded him to put it all down on paper. I needed it written – for the book.

Our conversation freaked me out. I expected him to beat around the bush for a while and then admit that Alice wasn't actually dead; that she'd come out of a coma twenty days later, but no one told him back then, or whatever crap a lying piece of shit would come up with. He never gave up on his initial version though. What if it's true? But then I think about it… Why would he back down? He was aware that I didn't have any social media accounts, nor did I have any desire to have any. It's definitely easier to lie about someone's death to a person who doesn't have social media.

Now I live with a constant feeling of concern deep down in my throat, but I must admit that if anything, this whole obscureness makes a nice ending to Alice's book.

On one hand, it lives up to her passion for discovering new worlds wherever we are. You know, regardless of what actually happened to her, in the world of Tino's friends, she's dead. Each reader can decide for themselves whether their Alice is still alive. Each reader can decide for themselves if they live in a world where life is predestined and fate gives us signs of what lies ahead.

The open ending also corresponds to her idea that life isn't a jigsaw puzzle but a construction set. It suggests that Alice doing certain stupid things at a certain stage of her youth doesn't determine anything. It doesn't mean she doomed herself to pieces of a jigsaw puzzle that would inevitably come together to form a tragic picture. She could have reached out for a better part of the construction set at any time; she could have changed her destiny a thousand times over. Having worked in the nightlife scene for so many years, I've seen a lot of girls into drugs. Alice could have built or ruined so many different scenarios. Tino's devastating story could be a total fabrication. Or perhaps things did happen more or less as he said, and Alice did overdose, but it didn't kill her. And then maybe she quit drugs after getting nearly killed. Maybe she graduated; stopped putting her feet up on the dashboard every time she traveled in a car; maybe she's suddenly happy with a "real" job and considering starting a family, as most of my friends close to thirty are doing. Many women find this age critical with regard to giving birth. Maybe Alice is no different. Of course, she could have already become a mother. Would she have ditched Boro if she got pregnant?

Or, she could've decided that she didn't want to have kids; that she'd rather travel the world.

Anything could have happened to Alice. The twenty-five-year-old flame that I knew was that kind of girl – anything could happen to her. A fine blend of traits that could either help her achieve greatness in life or make a complete failure out of her.

You might say: "Hey, this guy is contradicting himself! I thought he supported the theory that people's personalities are utterly predictable. So, how is it possible that Alice could be anything now?" Yes, this is a theory I believe in. But if you love someone too much, you can't know them perfectly well. Emotions always get in the way of your judgment. And there's something else too – when you know a person too deeply, when you've seen all the faces they've got, you start believing that they're capable of anything.

Most people will certainly take me for a horribly callous person for not having turned the world upside down in order to find out whether Alice is alive. It's just that… I've learned how to live with feelings of painful loss. Maybe you'll understand me if I answered this question that Alice asked me once: "What's with the pink laces on all your shoes?" Sharing this isn't easy, but Alice has always been so sincere, trusting everyone with her personal stuff, that I feel like I owe her this one.

Everyone has some past trauma that they wave about like a shield when people happen to call them crazy. In my case, I used to have a wife and a kid. We were too young when my wife got pregnant, and my initial reaction was to say that I wasn't ready for this step. As shameful as it sounds in hindsight, I secretly hoped she'd decide to have an abortion. However, she said: "No moment is perfectly right for having a kid. But no moment is perfectly wrong either." Despite everything that followed, I'm infinitely grateful to her for her decision. Because Emma, my daughter, was the most beautiful thing I've had in my life! The only perfection that I've ever created. In my memories she'll always be this little angel with dimples instead of wings… She'd just learned how to say "Hug, daddy;" I never got the chance to hear her say more complex words. Her mom and I fought all the time. I'd slowly learned that she was a mythomaniac; I kept discovering lie after lie… Eventually she even claimed that Emma wasn't mine. Then, using all sorts of schemes, she took Emma to live abroad. She didn't even leave me a picture of my daughter. The only thing she left behind was a pair of tiny sneakers with pink laces.

For a long time, I just walked around like a ghost. I ceaselessly imagined Emma saying "Hug, daddy" to a stranger. But it's true that every memory fades with time. Gradually, I thought about her less and less. One day I realized that I hadn't thought about Emma for days and I hated myself; eventually I couldn't even remember her face. That's why I changed the laces on my sneakers – to remind me.

I didn't want to share all this with Alice because she might have fallen for me even more. For all I know, she'd have decided that she needed to cure me. I told her that I wasn't capable of love, and to an extent that's true. Losing your child doesn't exactly make you a person who's interested in romantic feelings.

I hope Alice reads this and she's satisfied that she got the answer to at least one of her many questions. Questions and answers were a pain in the ass for her. Here's what she wrote on a couple of waitress notes when she contemplated the ending of the book:

In the intro I asked myself a lot of questions about people and about absurdities. Now, in conclusion, my questions have only increased. And they concern my own existence even more sharply. I'm lost, so lost in the cul-de-sacs of my mind.

What is home *exactly? Is it simply the place where my toothbrush lives? There's gotta be more to it! To a man who's obsessed with his mistresses and doesn't even notice his wife, the cheapest hotel room could feel like home. And what about me? I don't feel like I'm home anywhere.*

And what should I look for in a partner if I want to experience lasting happiness in a relationship? I've always imagined that the Perfect Guy will be gentle with me all the time, understand my emotions and all. But guys don't seem to work like that. It's rare to find a man who'll make sense of why I'm moved to tears at the sight of cute baby animals.

Maybe it's not about finding someone who understands. Maybe it's about accepting that they don't have to understand.

I need to find a way out of the Love-Work-Love cycle too; trying to forget the caress of every broken love by throwing myself into the arms of work, but then quickly abandoning all my plans for professional development as soon as I fall in love with yet another fragile ideal. An ideal that will be shattered to pieces again, sooner or later. And if it isn't, it just gets boring. And then I'm back to being a workaholic... How the hell do I break this vicious cycle of never accomplishing anything?

So many questions ... too many. My problem isn't that I can't find any answers; it's that the more you think, the more likely all of the potential answers seem. Or the more unlikely. You choose. It's exactly the same with repeating numbers – they could portend success, but they could also portend misery. You choose.

I guess that someday I'll find the truth. Cross my heart, I'll write Alice on a Saturday Morning *then. I'll write a new book, sober and sunny. On Friday night though, I still don't know shit.*

In my opinion, knowing isn't all that essential. Perhaps all of our confusion is just a paragraph in the Universe's marketing plan. Like the thing with shoes and car tires: even if companies could produce shoes and tires that never wear out, it's not profitable to do so. It's better for them if we need to buy new stuff every year. Perhaps the Universe planned it that way too: if we never find any answers, we're constantly broken and every year we develop a fresh interest in buying life's shit.

I'm sure that if Alice stops tormenting herself with questions, she'll be happy even without detailed information about what happiness is.

True power isn't bench pressing a hundred, or choking back tears when you need to let it all out, or wrapping people around your little finger, or not letting them wrap you around theirs. No. True power is allowing yourself to lose battles every now and then; falling into rabbit holes; crying when you hit the bottom... AND STILL LOVING YOUR LIFE AS IT IS, ON THIS WORLD AND NO OTHER.

I'll find out what has happened to Alice very soon. I need to find her; I figured I can't publish her work without her explicit permission (or her family's permission – in the gruesome case that I'd rather not think about). We'll need to settle the authorship too. Would she want to publish the book under her real name, or would she prefer to hide behind an alias?

I'm starting my search for her with something she'll like. In the style of her favorite Exupéry, I drew a picture, and now I ask:

Please, look at this girl carefully so that you will be sure to recognize her in case you go some night to The Mockingbird and she's there. If this should happen, please comfort me. Send me a word that she has come back.

I think I'm done here. I'll leave you with these last words of Alice:

Let me tell you something: YOU NEED TO BLOW IT ALL OUT!

Blow out those candles on your birthday cake! And while you're blowing, don't forget to make a wish! Wishes aren't the icing on the cake, they won't make you feel heavy. As for the fire, don't be afraid. You can't learn how to extinguish it without getting yourself burned.

Blow out the candles and dream as you used to when you were a child. Have you noticed that many kids want to be garbage men when they grow up? Children's dreams are like that – you can take them to pee by a tree on the main road. They won't blush like tomatoes and nobody will throw tomatoes at them either.

But then it all changes. By the time we've turned six, we are forced to pick a fig leaf and hide our nudity. And this is where we've got it all wrong. So, we've put our bikini tops on, but that doesn't mean our dreams have grown up along with us. Childhood dreams remain young forever. And when they want something from you, you can't just say no. All your life they'll cry inside, as sad as only a child can be. But if you bring them presents, they'll be overjoyed as only kids can be. And you'll be happy.

P.S. Make sure there are as many candles on the cake as there are years to your life. We tend to buy number-shaped candles these days, because it's easier. Well, number-shaped candles are for amateurs. You don't want to be an amateur when it comes to dreaming, do you?

Your Notes Here

Made in the USA
Monee, IL
07 October 2025

31701673R00152